Meet the comman...
The elite intelligen...

STARHAWKS

COMMANDER BRYAN KELLY. The Admiral's son whose early mission ended in disaster. *Valiant* is his chance to redeem himself . . .

DR. ANTOINETTE BEAULIEU. The brilliant but disillusioned ship's medic, she's already been forced out of the service once. She has a lot to prove.

CAESAR SAMMS. The only surviving member of Kelly's first command. He's tough, loyal, and battle-hardened—but his carefree lack of caution can ruin them all . . .

PHILA MOHATSA. The volatile junior operative whose secret past on a frontier planet has trained her in the use of exotic—and illegal—killing tools . . .

OLAF SIGGERSON. An older, more experienced civilian pilot, pressed into service, who rarely agrees with Commander Kelly's judgment.

OPERATIVE 41. The genetically altered half Salukan, dependable, but cold and impartial—who can be sure where his true alliance lies?

OUOJI. The ship's mascot . . . and perhaps much more.

FULL SPEED AHEAD—
ADVENTURE AWAITS!

OPERATION STARHAWKS

BOOK THREE

BEYOND THE VOID

SEAN DALTON

ACE BOOKS, NEW YORK

This book is an Ace original edition,
and has never been previously published.

BEYOND THE VOID

An Ace Book / published by arrangement with
the author

PRINTING HISTORY
Ace edition / January 1991

ISBN: 0-441-14156-0

Ace Books are published by The Berkley Publishing Group,
200 Madison Avenue, New York, New York 10016.
The name "ACE" and the "A" logo
are trademarks belonging to Charter Communications, Inc.

PRINTED IN THE UNITED STATES OF AMERICA

10 9 8 7 6 5 4 3 2 1

"All Special Operations personnel report to briefing room, level 17. All Special Operations personnel report to briefing room, level 17."

The message came over audio in the pool area of Station 4's recreational facilities.

In the main pool Commander Bryan Kelly had the wall lane. He broke his lap and heaved himself out, splashing pink-tinted water over 41, who had been watching him exercise with grave attention. Bronzed and lithe, with his blond mane of hair brushing his bare shoulders, 41 attracted plenty of attention from the female swimmers, but Kelly had yet to get 41 into the pool.

Now, he grinned in mock apology at his drenched friend. "Sorry. Hazards of sitting so close to the edge."

41 slicked his dripping hair back from his face and rose to his feet. "Swimming by choice is a waste of time."

Kelly stood up beside him and shook water from his ears. He felt sleek and warmed up from his exercise. "It's good for you. Keeps you from getting space flab."

41 squeezed his tawny eyes half shut in amusement. "There are other ways to avoid that. The summons sounded urgent."

"They're always urgent. Probably some report on a galactic invasion that we'll have to turn back single-handed. Or a lecture on correct ship hygiene procedures." Kelly jerked his thumb at the nearly empty pool. "It's quicker to cut across. Care to race?"

"No."

"Oh, come on, 41! I know you can swim. What's the problem?"

"I don't like to get wet."

Kelly grinned. "You're already wet. I'll bet you dinner at the Tokyo Club that I can beat you across."

"If you lose, you will be angry."

"No I won't. Hawks honor."

41 looked into his eyes a moment, then smiled. Without warning he turned and launched himself in a long, clean dive, shooting beneath the water like an arrow.

"Hey!" shouted Kelly.

He dived in, seeing 41's churning wake drawing even farther ahead, and forced himself not to surface before he had used the last of his dive impetus. Then he curved to the surface and went to work, stroking long, smooth, and fast. He hadn't been swimming champion of Buckstead and later of the Fleet Academy for nothing. And no amount of a head start was going to help 41 in this race.

41 had a peculiar stroke that Kelly had never seen before. It was choppy and looked like it wasted a lot of motion, but it was fast and it kept 41 ahead. Roughing it in 41's wake, Kelly's natural competitiveness made him draw on his kick although they were only halfway across the diagonal of the pool. He drew even with 41, keeping clear of those flailing arms.

A burn spread slowly through Kelly's muscles. He began to drag for breaths, feeling the effort under his rib cage with every stroke. Keep it smooth, he reminded himself. Don't start battling the water like 41.

But although he was giving his best, he couldn't draw ahead. They fought neck and neck for several meters. Kelly glimpsed the corner of the pool as a vague shadow ahead. He reached deep for whatever he had left and pulled ahead of 41, sucking air on every other stroke, his body a machine on fire, his heart pounding like an engine. But he still had it, and he felt the high of winning kick in.

Then 41 surged past him by a full length and touched the corner. Kelly's stroke faltered. He went under and came up again at the side of the pool, frowning as he slicked his black hair from his eyes.

41 was already crouched on the side, reaching down to give him a hand. Reluctantly, still not able to believe it, Kelly accepted the help. He sat on the side a moment, his legs dangling in the water, and panted for air.

Worse, 41 wasn't even breathing half as hard. He crouched on his haunches, muscles rippling under the tawny skin as he stretched. His golden hair lay sleeked against his narrow skull. Water streamed off him, leaving a puddle upon the paving.

"You suckered me," said Kelly between breaths. "I thought you could maybe dog paddle a little, but—"

"I knew you would be angry."

"No!" Kelly caught his arm before he could move away. "I'm not angry, just surprised. Where did you learn to swim like that? Your stroke looks like a mess, but it works. I'd like to learn it."

41 stared at him a long moment, impassive, summing him up. Then mischief lit his eyes and he cocked his head to one side. "Maybe one day I'll show you. But you owe me dinner. A big dinner." 41 smacked his lips. "I have an appetite for . . . oh, twelve courses at least."

Kelly put his hand over his eyes with a mock groan. "Did I say the Tokyo? I meant the bar and grill down on level—"

"You said Tokyo. The most expensive place on this station." 41 pulled Kelly to his feet. "I had to win the bet. I have no money to buy you dinner."

Kelly snorted. "Sure you do. You never buy anything. What do you do, hoard it all for a rainy day?"

41 frowned. "What does rain have to do with money?"

"It's just an expression. The way you save your salary, you're probably the richest person on the *Valiant*."

"No, it is Siggerson who hoards his salary. He even eats at the Commissary." 41 grinned, showing a dangerous set of teeth. "I want my expensive dinner now."

The lights overhead blinked twice, then a harsh klaxon sounded.

"Station Alert. Station Alert. Station Alert."

A few desultory swimmers who'd been watching Kelly and 41 race now scrambled from the pool. The lights dimmed to a mere glow, causing Kelly and 41 to bump into each other as they reached for towels. A woman strode by, dripping water and cursing steadily to herself. Behind them, a steel deck began closing over the surface of the pools.

"Hell," said Kelly, glancing around as they joined the small crowd exiting the area. "I've never seen a station under attack before."

"What is our duty?" asked 41.

"Report to the *Valiant*."

"And the order to go to briefing?"

Kelly draped his towel across his neck and began to jog down the corridor. "If we're under attack, I'm not letting my ship be bottled up in the hangar. Come on!"

Station 4 was a miniature city, self-contained within a hull of pyrillium alloy. Possessing one hundred six levels in addition to its vast hangar facilities, it was fitted with free enterprise shops, casinos, bars, restaurants, concert halls, sporting arenas, recreation facilities to suit the varied needs of the Allied Species, two museums, a library, sophisticated medical and therapy units, and five training centers. Civilians were permitted access to the station, but it remained a military installation, and housed the headquarters of the Special Operations branch of the Allied Intelligence Agency.

Most of the time the station looked like an attractive resort. Now, however, with battle lighting on and crimson warnings flashing at each corridor intersection, it was all business. Featureless walls became data screens. Computer optics flashed on. Personnel lined up at their stations, keying in commands that scrolled data.

Kelly paused at an unmanned screen and touched his hand to the square beneath it. A keypad lit beneath the heat of his fingertips. He tapped in a command for visual and a harsh beep canceled his command. The screen blanked and the keypad disappeared.

"Damn," said Kelly. "I don't know the approach range before the station raises its shields. Once they're up, we can't get out."

41 tried to use a public comm, snarled something incomprehensible, and caught up with Kelly who was hurrying on. "Inoperable. What about the squad?"

"There's no time to track them down now," said Kelly.

The hangar area had been sealed, but Kelly's IDent card, which he wore on a chain around his neck, overrode the lock and they got admittance. They hurried down the access corridor, which curved in a long semicircle around the docking facilities. The glass wall on the inside curve showed suited maintenance crews swarming over at least four of the half-dozen ships at dock. Crews in a myriad of uniforms swarmed the corridor, and there were plenty of glances at Kelly and 41 in their swim trunks.

Kelly didn't see any Hawks in the crowd. Furiously he strode down an offshoot passageway to the minor berths where the *Valiant* rested, gleaming white from a hull bath and replating. He rammed his IDent card into the lock and fumed impatiently while the code cycled through.

"West and his damned briefings," said Kelly. The light on the lock glowed green, and he jerked out his card.

"Every Fleeter on this station will be out there in the action in a matter of minutes, and where're Kestrel and Harrier? Sitting on their tails on level 17."

The airlock opened and he strode inside, followed by 41. They were sprayed with decontaminants, then the inner lock opened and Kelly was aboard the *Valiant*, a trim little proto-class cruiser powered by photonic drive. The interior lights came on automatically as sensors registered their presence. 41 veered off toward the engine area. Kelly climbed the ladder to the quarterdeck.

Emerging from the turnaround, he saw his pilot, Olaf Siggerson, slumped in a chair with a complicated computer game displayed on the main viewscreen. Ouoji, the ship's mascot, lay curled up in his lap. Her blue eyes opened wide at Kelly's appearance, and with a graceful bound, she came running to bump her head against his leg in greeting.

Kelly petted her briefly. "Hello, Ouoji. Siggerson, I'm not even going to ask you what you're doing spending your leave on board. Get the engines warmed up double-speed."

Siggerson—lanky, balding, and freckled—frowned and canceled his game. He moved to his master station and activated the boards.

"What's up?" he asked. "New orders? I need to cancel a dinner appointment—"

"Haven't you kept a line open to the station?" asked Kelly, calling up data reports on the ship's status. She'd been overhauled and refitted. She was ready. "We're under a station alert. All hell's breaking loose. And I want to be out of here before the shields go up."

Siggerson blinked, and his usually unshakable calm broke. "Station alert? Do you mean we're being attacked? Here? By whom?"

"I can't find out," said Kelly in frustration.

Siggerson activated the viewscreen and observed the chaos raging outside. Audio brought in the calm computer tones of the hangar: "Attention. Hangar doors now opening. Attention."

"I can't get anything beyond the station. Too much interference," said Siggerson. "Engines almost ready for cast off."

"Good." Kelly paced around the quarterdeck. "I want to be ready to move the moment we can."

"Requesting cast off now. It'll take a minute or two for the request to be routed."

"Forget normal procedures! Can't you override and give the cast off order from here?"

"No," said Siggerson. "It's a security feature, to keep the ship from being stolen."

"Oh, for—"

"There are ways around security features," said a crisp, feminine voice.

Phila Mohatsa emerged from the turnaround, garbed in a crimson jumpsuit. Her black, curly hair flowed loose over her shoulders. She took a second look at Kelly in his swim trunks, and smiled in approval. To his embarrassment he felt his face flush.

"I figured you guys would come here. *Vita mandale*, right?" She laughed, tossing back her hair, and took her station at communications. "Let me see what I can do that's illegal."

"Give me a call the minute we get clearance," said Kelly. "I'm going to check stores." And get some clothes on, he added mentally.

"Right," said Siggerson without looking up from his work. "By the way, Commander—"

"Yes?"

"If Mohatsa gets us loose, I'll have to do free piloting out through this traffic. That means about thirty violations slapped on us, providing I don't have a wreck."

Kelly met Siggerson's eyes. Siggerson was always a stickler down to the last detail. He also happened to be one of the best pilots in the business.

"You won't have a wreck," said Kelly with a smile. "Leave the violations to me."

"Kelly charm, I suppose," said Siggerson grouchily.

Phila laughed. "No, his daddy is an admiral, remember? I just severed the security code. Stand by for your cast off order."

"Standing by," said Siggerson.

Kelly let the gibes pass. He'd asked for them when he gave the orders to cut security. Heading down the ladder with an ever-curious Ouoji draped upon his shoulder, he met Caesar coming up.

Warm relief flooded Kelly. For a moment he was simply grateful to his squad. Starting nearly a year ago as a mismatched bunch of arguing operatives, they'd molded themselves into a crack team that knew what to do and when. Best of all, in an emergency they all came home to the *Valiant*.

He gripped Caesar's shoulder, unable to speak for a moment.

"Boss, hold up old Siggie for a few minutes, will you?" said Caesar, puffing. His red hair was dark with sweat at the roots and his eyes were bloodshot. He reeked of liquor and smoke and Othian musk. Kelly didn't even want to imagine what kind of den Caesar had been socializing in. "We're trying to get the stores loaded, but it's damned hot in the hold with the engines on warm up and I figure Siggie's going to blast out of here any minute without checking his hatch closings."

"You figured right," said Kelly as Ouoji transferred herself to Caesar's shoulder with a wipe of her long, bushy tail under Kelly's nose. She sniffed Caesar and chittered angrily.

He clamped a hand on her muzzle. "Yeah, yeah. I been having a good time, and I don't need *you* moralizing to *me*, fur face."

She clamped her ear openings flat to her round skull and jumped down in a huff.

"Siggerson and Phila are working on getting us cast off,"

said Kelly. "There isn't much time for loading. What do you have for stores?"

"It's a grab bag. I just appropriated a grav-flat full of stuff on the way. No one is watching anything right now. All the technicians are running their butts off trying to get the battle cruisers ready."

Caesar led Kelly down the ladder with a grin. Only a slight unsteadiness in his walk betrayed that he was less than fully sober. They went into the minuscule hold where 41 was heaving canisters and boxes around in an effort to make everything fit.

"Mostly weapons and some food," said Caesar in satisfaction. He tapped a crate stamped PRIVATE STORES. "What's this? Got the *Jefferson*'s emblem on it. Guess all this belongs to them."

41 paused in his work, sweat oiling his bare torso. "It's brandy, Earth manufacture."

Kelly and Caesar stared at the crate, urgency momentarily forgotten.

"Brandy," whispered Caesar in reverence.

Kelly recovered first. He glanced up. "You don't manufacture brandy. It's—"

"It's the breath of the gods," said Caesar, his green eyes aglow. "Oh, boss, what a haul."

"You'd better haul your—"

An entry request came from the airlock. Caesar and 41 resumed work and Kelly touched the comm.

"Somebody let me in!" snapped Dr. Beaulieu's voice. "I don't have my IDent with me and two hulking brutes from security are coming my way. If you don't—"

Kelly hit the release, and she abruptly cut off. Seconds later she was inside, looking unexpectedly beautiful and exotic in a flowing caftan that set off her coffee-colored skin. A cap of purple silk trimmed with gold perched atop her close-cropped hair. Gold bracelets covered her forearms and she carried a pouch bag of supple purple leather.

"That was close," she said, and hit the lock. Like Phila,

she took a second look at Kelly. "Well, I guess I don't have to worry about being without my uniform."

Before Kelly could answer, 41 appeared, bronzed and sweaty in his trunks.

"Everything is in place," 41 said, oblivious to Beaulieu's stare. "Siggerson flashed a request for you on the quarterdeck."

"That means he's got cast off." Kelly glanced around at them. "Everybody, upstairs. Get strapped in. I don't know what we're getting into, but it's going to be lively."

They filed down the corridor, and Kelly added, "Sorry about the end of your leave."

41 went into his cabin without comment. Caesar looked rueful, but Beaulieu said briskly, "To be frank, Commander, anything has to be better than dying of boredom at a Brahms concert with an elderly escort who *gropes*."

"Was it the music that was boring, or the escort?" asked Caesar with a wicked grin.

"Both," she retorted. She fished in her pouch and brought out a small packet. "Chew up this tablet. It'll get you sober."

"Who wants to be—"

Kelly ducked into his cabin and grabbed some clothes. By the time he reached the quarterdeck, the viewscreen showed that they were moving. Everyone quickly strapped themselves in place, and Kelly glanced at Mohatsa's station.

"Are we being hailed, Phila?"

"Insistently. They're also trying to beam a scrambler into our systems and stop us." Phila's dark eyes flashed. "It's a good thing we rigged our own security codes into this baby."

"Clearing berth," said Siggerson without looking up.

The large astrogation screen in the center of the horseshoe seating area lit up. Against the soft green backdrop, white blips appeared. Kelly studied it a moment.

"You've got the whole hangar graphed out."

"Don't want any collisions," said Siggerson.

"Commander," said Mohatsa. "We're being hailed by the ESS *Jefferson*."

The big starship was coming into range on their viewscreen now. She was already halfway out the hangar doors, and from this angle Kelly could see the blackened side of her lower decks where she'd taken Salukan fire in a recent skirmish. Her captain had reported casualties. She must be going out at half power, with half a crew's complement. But she was going.

Old pride in the fleet caught Kelly in the throat. He said, "Respond to their hail."

"Yes sir."

The viewscreen changed to show them the bridge of the *Jefferson*. Captain Lewis, craggy-faced with bristling eyebrows and eyes the color of steel, glared at them from the screen.

"What the hell do you think you're doing, *Valiant*? You can't pilot free through this traffic."

"I'm Commander Kelly. We have the capability, and we can be of assistance. Are you registering what is approaching the station?"

"Not yet," said Lewis. "These damned Minzanese engineers have us jammed with all their infernal shielding. My science officer assures me that we'll have full sensor capabilities in about twenty-five seconds. In the meantime we have to sail out of here blind. Damned stupid arrangement. Whoever designed this station ought to have his butt kicked to Boxcan."

"Will you transmit that sensor data to us?" asked Kelly.

"The hell I will! You're not even in the Fleet—"

Something broke up the transmission. Lewis' face became dancing black dots. Then the screen blanked. Mohatsa put the hangar visual back on.

Kelly set his jaw in irritation. "Phila, can you pirate off his sensors? He may be willing to go out of here blind, but I'm not."

She grinned at the challenge. "Can do."

Beaulieu leaned forward with a small frown. "Isn't that illegal?"

Kelly shrugged and Caesar said, "After the little stunt we're doing now, what're a few more broken laws going to hurt?"

In a few moments the data came in. Transmission was patchy, but as the *Jefferson* cleared the station and switched to long-range sensors, the *Valiant's* viewscreen showed hazy, distorted space.

"I see it!" said Caesar, pointing at the top left corner of the screen. "Formation. Enemy ships approaching."

"What's their speed?" asked Kelly.

"I can't read it," replied Phila.

Magnification improved as though the people on the *Jefferson* were trying to refine their data. Kelly leaned forward, squinting at the tiny blips. Too far for positive identification. But there was something odd about them. He frowned. Where had he seen a formation like that before?

"Alien formation. Not Fleet," said Caesar.

Kelly glanced at Siggerson. "Get us out of this hangar."

"I'm trying," said Siggerson, glued to his instruments. Droplets of sweat shone on his forehead. "Those two frigates are being tractored out. If we cross one of those beams, it could crack our hull."

The strut of a starship passed in front of their sensors, blurring on the main viewscreen. Kelly looked hastily away. They were taking a horrible risk of collision. Probably every captain present was cursing them.

"The station is sending out a powerful hailing frequency to those ships," said Phila. "They do not respond."

"No wonder the alert went up," said Caesar. "I'd better check our bomb hatches. We've never used them, and this is a hell of a time to find out if they work."

"I will help," said 41, following him off the quarterdeck.

The *Valiant* suddenly lurched, flipping Ouoji off the helm console. She twisted deftly in the air and landed on her feet, switching her tail angrily. Kelly glanced at Siggerson, who said, tight-lipped, "Had to apply the brakes. Continuing."

Beaulieu turned away from the viewscreen. "I can't watch this."

Kelly turned his attention back to Phila's small viewer and those enemy ships. They were much closer now, yet not close enough for a visual identification. If she wanted, the *Jefferson* could deploy extended-range missiles within another minute.

The second starship in the hangar had cleared the doors. Siggerson lined up the *Valiant* between the second frigate and a scoutship, nudging too close for safety margins.

"Do you think the Salukans would dare penetrate this far into Alliance space?" asked Phila. "Risk all-out war? Those ships are too large for anything the Jostics have. And they're showing too much discipline to be a raid."

"They aren't Salukans," said Kelly. "That isn't a Salukan formation. It's . . . Damn! I've seen that somewhere before. I know I have."

"Look how they're bunched together. I count six ships, destroyer-class size at least," said Phila, tapping the screen with her finger. "Everything else is too muddy. As soon as we're clear, I can use our own sensors. The *Jefferson* has muck for equipment."

"Hang on," said Siggerson. "This is going to be dicey."

Kelly glanced over his shoulder at the main viewscreen in time to see them suddenly jockey past the scoutship that was trying to cut them off. The *Valiant* turned on her side and shot through the hangar doors with less than a meter to spare.

"Warning!" said the computer's voice. "Craft is too close to hangar doors. Warning! Craft is—"

"We're through!" said Siggerson, and the *Valiant* swooped up and over the top of a frigate so close Kelly had a dizzying view of its upper running lights before they cleared.

"Good work!" said Kelly, and turned back to Phila's screen.

She cleared the pirate link off the *Jefferson*'s sensors, and the quality improved at once as their own, longer-range sensors took up the job.

"Those are Fleet destroyers," said Phila in puzzlement. "I don't understand. What are they doing, approaching us from that direction, without standard hailing procedures, in an unknown formation? Can the Salukans have designed them as a trick?"

Kelly didn't answer. He was staring hard at the screen. He had seen that formation before. Long ago, when he was a child.

The answer snapped into his mind. Kelly straightened. "Those are our ships," he said. "They must be disabled, their communications cut off. That formation is their way of telling us they won't attack."

"How do you know that?" said Phila, glancing up at him. "Looks pretty *cosquenti* to me."

"My father and I used to play strategy games when I was a young boy. I had an old discarded military mapboard that lit up with about six fleets. So I could have hundreds of ships in motion if I chose." Excitedly Kelly pointed at the screen. "That formation was one we invented. Broken wing formation! It meant we were coming in wounded, without communications, and needed help."

"Are you sure?" said Siggerson doubtfully.

"Yes, I'm sure. My father must be out there in that squadron. It's coming from the direction of Nielson's Void, isn't it? They must have been on maneuvers, and something's gone wrong. Phila, get me a line to Captain Lewis."

"You've got it, Commander."

"Kelly!" shouted Lewis in a fury. "You damned fool! You've broken every regulation in the book, and I don't care which book it is! What the hell are you doing out here in the way?"

"Captain, those are not enemy ships," said Kelly urgently, gripping the back of Phila's chair until his knuckles turned white. "It's a Fleet squadron—"

"Nonsense. Fleet squadrons have five destroyers apiece. We've identified six ships. They're Salukan mock-ups, designed to fool us into letting them approach. But I—"

"Sir, you must listen to me. Don't fire on them. They're ours—"

"Have you established contact with them?" asked Lewis.

Kelly frowned. "No, sir."

"Then don't tell me how to do my business. They are coming down a closed space lane. They have answered no hailing frequencies. They have not identified themselves to Station 4 or made approach requests. They are not flying in a specific Fleet formation. Therefore, they must be stopped. Regulations—"

"Don't quote regulations," snapped Kelly. "I'm telling you that I recognize this formation! It's used for—"

"Son, I've been in the fleet for forty years," said Lewis. "Now shut up and get out of the way."

"*Jefferson* is preparing to fire long-extensions," said Siggerson.

"They've broken contact," said Phila.

Kelly punched the back of her chair with his fist. "Damn! Can we override their weaponry systems?"

Phila's eyes widened. "Negative."

"Firing . . . now," said Siggerson.

Kelly whirled. Feeling sick with helplessness, he watched the astrogation board chart the missiles' trajectories.

Extended-range missiles were antiquated and not expected to achieve much damage in delivering fire to the enemy. They could be easily destroyed in mid-flight before ever reaching their target. However, they were used primarily as warnings off or as a means to draw the enemy's fire and thus gauge the range and power of the enemy's weapons. But if their target was disabled and could not fire back . . .

"Intercept those missiles and destroy them," said Kelly.

For a moment only silence answered him. Beaulieu, Phila, and Siggerson all stared at him.

Phila reached out. "If you're wrong, Commander, you're finished."

"We'll all be finished with you," said Siggerson. "Charges of treason will be the least of—"

"Damn it! Do you trust me, or not?" shouted Kelly. "That's a direct order, Mr. Siggerson. You can protest it and stand down from your station, thus giving the controls to me. Or you can carry out your orders. But do one or the other *now*."

Siggerson's angular face looked bleached under the lights. He hesitated one second longer, then brushed his hand over his controls.

"Plotting an intercept course now. Prepare for distort. ETA six minutes at TD 7."

2

Kelly tensed, watching intently as Siggerson swooped them onto an intercept course. He called Caesar on the in-ship comm.

"Do the weapons systems check out? We're going to need them."

"Uh, right, boss," replied Caesar's voice. "Everything's clear. You need us back up there or—"

"No. Strap down tight."

Siggerson rolled the ship in a tight spin and they jumped into distort. Kelly lost his footing and went tumbling wildly across the quarterdeck. Winded and bruised, he scrambled to his chair at the first chance and strapped in.

Beaulieu shot him a grim look. In spite of her restraint harness, she was gripping the edge of her seat with both hands. "I should have dosed everyone for *mal d'espace*," she said, glaring at Siggerson. "I didn't know we were going to do an acrobatic show for the benefit of the Fleet. Are you all right, Commander?"

"Yes," said Kelly, still breathless. The viewscreen corrected for the blur effect of time distortion. Kelly watched the running missiles intently. "Distance, Phila?"

"Seventy-five hundred meters and closing."

Kelly leaned forward until the straps of his harness cut into his chest. "Can you detonate them electronically?"

Phila checked. "Uh, negative."

"Damn," said Kelly softly. "Can we nudge them off course?"

"Possible—"

Siggerson snorted. "They'd just correct it. We'll have to destroy those missiles. But our firepower isn't strong enough to crack their shielding."

"Sir!" said Phila urgently. "*Jefferson* is locking cannon onto us. They've sent a warning for us to veer off or they'll fire on us."

"Raise shields!" said Kelly, wishing he could use the waver. But the *Jefferson* could see right through it. "Siggerson, we can overtake the missiles and leave a mine in their path."

"Yes, but we'll cut it fine—"

A shudder rocked the *Valiant*, setting the lights flickering erratically for several seconds.

"Shields holding," said Phila.

"Do we continue?" asked Siggerson.

Kelly set his jaw. "That was just a little potshot. Continue, Mr. Siggerson."

"Sir," said Phila worriedly. "If they use stronger cannon fire, they could weaken our shields and even destroy them. We can't go head to head with a battle cruiser."

"Veer to feint course," said Kelly as though he had not heard. He called Caesar. "Are you still standing by in the hold?"

"Yeah, boss," said Caesar cheerfully. "We nearly got bounced on our skulls though. Who's shooting at us?"

"The *Jefferson*."

"What—"

"Listen," said Kelly sharply. "I want you to prepare for

manual release of mines one and three on my order. Siggerson's got too much to do up here without handling weapons."

"Can do. Standing by."

Keeping the line open, Kelly checked their distance and speed. Siggerson was looping in a wide trajectory meant to fool the *Jefferson* as to their increase in speed. And meanwhile the disabled squadron was drawing ever closer. They were within range now to destroy the missiles, but they did nothing. Kelly imagined the captains of those six ships watching their sensor data and feeling helpless. And if his father was on board one of those ships . . .

Swiftly Kelly brushed the worry away. He had to think now without any emotions clouding his judgment.

Siggerson dropped the *Valiant* four hundred meters and sent her arrowing right across the flight path of the lead missile. The *Jefferson* did not fire at them a second time. They could hardly do so now without taking the chance of hitting the missiles.

Kelly's stomach knotted with tension. The missile filled the viewscreen, coming right at them, seemingly too fast to miss. "Faster," he breathed. "Faster."

He waited, however, ignoring his own jumping nerves while he counted carefully the lag time. His finger touched the comm. "Fire one," he said.

The *Valiant* rocked slightly from the ejection. The viewscreen showed the mine tumbling in their wake. The missile struck it dead on. A brilliant fireball flashed across the screen, which could not dim quickly enough. Beaulieu covered her eyes, and Kelly swiftly averted his face.

"Preparing for second pass," said Siggerson.

Kelly blinked the dancing purple spots from his eyes. "Bull's-eye, Caesar. Good work."

"Ready when you are," said Caesar.

Siggerson brought the *Valiant* around and aimed her across the path of the second missile. They were almost in position when Phila whirled in her seat.

"Sir—"

The ship lurched as though slapped aside by a giant hand. Gravity and life support cut out along with the lights for what must have been only a few seconds. But to Kelly, floating against his harness and feeling as though he couldn't draw a breath, it seemed like an eternity. Then lights, heat, and air returned. But gravity remained off. One data screen near Philia's head flashed gibberish as though its computer had blown. Kelly could smell circuits burning somewhere.

"Shields . . . down," said Phila, coughing.

Fury caught Kelly in the throat. "Where are we?" he shouted, staring at the viewscreen that had gone crazy and wasn't relaying anything but visual static. "Where's that missile?"

"We were knocked out of its path. Close shooting," said Siggerson. "Their gunnery officer took a chance at that angle of shaving off the nose of the missile—"

"Siggerson!" shouted Beaulieu, her voice raw with reaction. "Who the hell cares how good a shot they are? We just got our pants scorched."

A pulse was beating hard in Kelly's temple. He gestured at Phila. "Open a line to Lewis."

Within seconds the viewscreen cleared and Captain Lewis' craggy features filled it. "Ready to surrender yourself for treason, Commander?" said Lewis.

Kelly's jaw was so taut it hurt to open his mouth. With all the will he possessed, he kept himself from screaming at the captain. "Firing on a fellow vessel without just cause is a worse offense, Lewis. You have no reason to shoot at that squadron *or* at us."

"The time is past for quibbling," said Lewis with a glower. "I know my job. I work by the book."

"You idiot!" shouted Kelly. "If that missile hits one of those ships, you'll be guilty of murder. Look at them! They've had plenty of time to shoot that missile to bits and they haven't done it. Doesn't that tell you they're helpless?"

"I have made my decision according to my best judgment and training," said Lewis heavily. "If you attempt to interfere again, Commander, you will be treated again as the enemy."

"I'm not going to let you compound this blundering," said Kelly. "Cut it, Phila."

Lewis' face vanished, showing them space once again. The missile was dangerously close to the leading destroyer of the squadron. From this angle, Kelly could now see that it was towing one of the other ships on a tractor beam. The towed ship's lower hull was dangerously crumpled. He saw other indications of damage along the line in twisted struts, blackened engine drives, broken conning towers. Phila increased magnification, and the registry names sprang at him: ESS *Sounder*, ESS *Dragon*, ESS *Fortya*, MSS *Omu Dar*, MSS *Omu Hochu*, ESS *Kelso*.

"They've been in one rough fight," said Phila.

"Look at that," said Siggerson, gazing openmouthed at the screen. "They're all linked together with tractor beams."

"Yeah," said Phila. "Only one ship is registering engine power. It must be pulling the whole mass. Commander, I'm reading life signs. Full crew complements. Still no communications. Life support looks iffy in spots."

Kelly clenched his fists. "Siggerson, we've got to make another pass and stop that missile. It's heading right for the powered ship."

"We still have the speed. We may lose heat as well as gravity on the way. Something has shorted."

"Do it," said Kelly.

The *Valiant* picked up speed with an unusual vibration running through her decks. It set Kelly's teeth on edge, but he did his best to ignore the sensation.

"Hey, boss?" said Caesar over the comm. "Are we done having our cage rattled?"

"No," said Kelly grimly. "We are making another pass."

"Oh. Firing tube three is jammed, I think. Uh, 41 says it

may blow out backward into our laps down here if we try to shoot it."

"Sir," said Phila, and her voice wasn't quite steady. "*Jefferson* is locking onto us again. We still have no shields."

Kelly hesitated. No command decision was ever fair. That was why officers couldn't sleep at night. But now, as he looked at the faces of his squad—worried, doubtful, yet *trusting* faces—he wondered if he was doing the right thing. Could Lewis be right? After all, Kelly was placing everything on one childhood memory. It could be strictly coincidental that these ships had come up out of nowhere in that formation . . .

"Commander," said Phila. "I'm getting a faint signal from the squadron. It's weak and full of break up . . . sounds like it's a wrist communicator."

Kelly unsnapped his harness and let himself float over to her station. "Put it on audio. Boost it all you can."

". . . emergency. Earthship *Sounder* calling oncoming vessels. Call off . . . attack . . . damaged. Can't steer—"

"Could be a faked message," said Beaulieu. They all stared at her, and she added, "If Lewis is right."

"That old croaker!" began Phila indignantly.

Kelly gestured. "Open a channel on that frequency." As soon as Phila nodded, Kelly said, "This is Commander Kelly of the MSS *Valiant*. We read you, *Sounder*. But you are approaching a space station on a closed space lane without authorization or identification. Can you identify yourselves more definitely?"

He stopped speaking and grimaced, his mouth dry as he watched the missile closing on the helpless ships. He could imagine the chain reaction that would occur when it struck. One exploding vessel at such close range would explode the others. And yet . . . he had to be sure before he laid the lives of his crew on the line.

"*Sounder* to *Valiant*," replied a voice that despite the static sent shivers down Kelly's spine. "This is Admiral

Kelly, commanding Red Squadron back from classified maneuvers in Nielson's Void. Repeat . . . Kelly . . . back from . . . Broken wing formation—"

"I *knew* it!" shouted Kelly. He let out a shrill whoop. "Siggerson, put us on intercept. Phila, launch our log recording. Get everyone assembled in the teleport bay. On the double!"

Beaulieu unsnapped her harness and floated tentatively free. "Teleport?" she said. "Why?"

But it was Siggerson, ashen-faced, who answered for Kelly. "You're going to let the missile hit the *Valiant*. Kelly, you can't!"

It was the cry of a man in anguish. Kelly knew how deeply Siggerson loved this little ship. He knew it was the *Valiant* that kept Siggerson loyal to them, for Siggerson had joined the Hawks for no other reason than to pilot her. But Kelly had other loyalties that ran deeper.

"We're doing it," said Kelly in a voice that allowed no argument. "Go, Beaulieu. Phila."

"Launching the log now," she said, her voice small and tight. She scrambled from her chair and shot expertly across the quarterdeck to the turnaround. She went down the ladder headfirst.

Kelly floated, one hand hanging onto the corner of the helm console. "Set the course and program her to stop in the missile's path," he said.

Siggerson stared at him with eyes like milky glass. Blinking, he finally dropped his gaze and complied. "Go ahead, Kelly," he said in a choked voice. "I'll finish the task, then report to—"

"No. Clear the quarterdeck."

Red flooded Siggerson's face. He glared at Kelly, but Kelly never relented an inch. Slowly, reluctantly, Siggerson unsnapped his harness and pushed himself off from his chair.

"There's got to be another way. I could find it—"

"We don't have time," said Kelly. "Move."

He launched himself from the console and as he passed Siggerson, he grabbed the pilot by the arm and let his impetus pull Siggerson along. When he bumped gently into the turnaround, he hooked his right leg over the top to stabilize himself and pushed Siggerson toward the ladder.

"There'll be other ships," said Kelly. "Don't be a fool. Move!"

"You know there won't," said Siggerson as he went down the ladder. "You'll be busted for this, and we'll all go down with you. I'll be lucky if I can get signed onto an ore freighter."

"Hey, Siggie! Complaining again?" called Caesar's cheerful voice from the lower deck. "Boss, I hear we're teleporting over to the main target."

"Right," said Kelly, reaching the end of the ladder and pushing off down the corridor.

Caesar whistled. "Great. Looks like we can get blown to smithers here or go over to the other ships and be blown to—"

"We've got about four minutes to teleport," said Kelly.

Caesar turned pale and abruptly shut up.

In the small teleport bay, Phila and Beaulieu had their wristbands on and were crouched on the platform, holding themselves on the contact points with their hands. 41 was floating up near the ceiling in one corner, wrestling to fasten a band on Ouoji who was struggling with angry lashings of her tail. She squawled loudly.

"What are you doing to her?" said Siggerson. He grabbed Kelly's shoulder and launched himself up toward 41. "Let me do that. You're just frightening her."

Kelly touched the controls and Phila and Beaulieu shimmered out. Caesar sent a wristband floating his way, and Kelly wedged his knee into a corner of the control board to hold himself in place while he fastened it on.

"Siggerson!" he said sharply. "Get down here and prepare for teleport."

41 planted his feet on the ceiling and gave Siggerson a

push down. Siggerson held the unhappy Ouoji cradled in his arms. Her blue eyes were slitted, and her ear flaps were clamped tight. She squawled again, a low, eerie cry of rage and fear. Since Siggerson couldn't take a chance on releasing her, Caesar put a band on his wrist for him.

"Guess the little fur face hasn't had her freefall training," said Caesar with a grin. He maneuvered Siggerson onto the platform and got on with him. His thumbs-up gesture was the last of him to shimmer from existence.

"Get down here," said Kelly to 41, who was still floating near the ceiling. "We've got about forty-five seconds."

41 moved in zero gravity as though he had been born to it. He got into position on the platform as Kelly joined him.

"The automatic controls are always slower than the manual says."

Kelly looked at him in surprise. "You've been reading the ship's manuals? Why?"

"To learn. I have no science training. When there is trouble with the ship, as now, I cannot help much."

Kelly thought about 41 gravely plowing through the heavy technical material in the manuals and started to tell 41 that there were easier ways to learn the skills he was seeking when an explosion rocked the ship. The lights cut out, and Kelly was conscious of an enormous roaring sound that engulfed him along with tremendous heat.

41 said something that he couldn't make out, then there came the familiar nausea and sense of displacement that told him the teleport had engaged. But if it would send them correctly or leave them in limbo as the power failed, he had no way of knowing.

Until he came to on a thinly cushioned steel deck, feeling as though he had been drop kicked. He opened his eyes, focused on nothing, closed them long enough to feel a nasty headache coming on, and opened his eyes again. This time the blurs around him became shapes with color and motion. He blinked and rubbed his eyes, and the shapes became

people with faces and uniforms. Human people, not Salukans or Jostics. Relief melted through him.

A hand gripped his arm. "Awaken," said 41. "We are in
trouble."

Kelly shook the webs from his mind and pulled himself
together. He sat up, muffling a groan, and let 41 haul him
to his feet.

Around him was a curved corridor of Fleet gray, plain
and slightly cramped. Kelly remembered long-ago days of
Fleet service and overcame the urge to stoop slightly
beneath the low ceilings.

Facing him and 41 were three young ensigns and a female
lieutenant. Smoke-smudged and red-eyed, their faces had
the grimness of battle fatigue. Their eyes held horror and
grief.

The lieutenant stepped forward. "Welcome aboard the
Sounder, Commander. All your people arrived intact.
You're wanted on the bridge. Would you come with us,
please?"

Words, pared down to the essentials, delivered in a voice
of weariness. In silence Kelly and 41 followed their escort.
As they walked Kelly noted the exposed panels and blackened traces of electrical fires. Cables as thick as his arm
hung from the ceiling in places. He could hear dangerous
humming inside as he ducked warily beneath them.

A lift whose door did not completely shut rose jerkily to
the bridge. Kelly stepped off to find himself in the gloom of
battle lighting. Crimson, green, and amber glowed from
data boards and tactical displays around him. The narrow,
rectangular bridge was crammed with equipment and the
crew manning it. At the far end stood two officers, a man
and a woman. Their backs were to Kelly for they faced the
large viewscreen that looked like a window onto space.
Stars glittered in a backdrop to the motley flotilla com-
manded by Captain Lewis.

But Kelly didn't care about the view. His gaze went to the

man whose back he could have recognized anywhere, anytime.

"Dad?" he whispered.

The admiral turned sharply. A full head taller than anyone on the bridge except for Kelly and 41, he was a handsome man with piercing blue eyes and thick silver hair cropped short military style. In his mid-sixties, he was as lean and fit as a man half his age, and his step always had a spring in it.

A smile touched his aquiline features briefly, and the look in his eyes warmed Kelly through. He stuck out his hand according to Fleet custom, and Kelly shook it with a grin.

"I knew it," he said. "As soon as I saw the formation on the viewscreen, I remembered our old strategy games."

"Pity your colleagues didn't believe you," said the admiral. He kept drinking Kelly in with his eyes. It had been two years since they had last met face-to-face. But with Lewis and company bearing down upon them, it wasn't much of a time for reunions.

Kelly stared at the viewscreen with disgust. "They're still coming? Can't they understand anything! Damn! I won't believe we sacrificed the *Valiant* for nothing."

As he spoke he glanced at Siggerson, standing wedged in a corner, looking lost.

The admiral cleared his throat. "Yes, well, you pulled quite a spectacular stunt out there, but now you're stuck with us. I take it you disobeyed orders?"

"Orders!" said Kelly scornfully. "Lewis is a fool. He proclaimed himself in charge, but he has as much business commanding a starship as our Ouoji."

"Meanwhile they're still coming," said the woman officer. "Any ideas as to what we might do now?"

She wore a gray uniform tunic with captain's bars on her collar. Close to Kelly's own age, she was blond and gray-eyed, with a lean, strong-featured face and tiny lines starting to carve themselves around her eyes.

"Captain," said the admiral. "I'd like to introduce Commander Bryan Kelly. Captain Aurie Serula."

Kelly shook hands and found hers dry and hard-gripped. She looked as tired as her crew. Her lovely, wide-set eyes were hollow as though she had seen more than anyone should.

"With two Kellys on board, we can't lose," she said. "Welcome to what's left of the *Sounder*."

"What we need," said Kelly, "is some decent communications."

"One of your operatives has tackled that project," said Serula with a shrug. She spoke Glish with the lilting accent of the Rim colonies. "We've been working on it for days with not much result."

Kelly glanced around the crowded bridge and finally spotted Phila and Caesar conferring together over a tangled mess of a circuit panel. He smiled and returned his gaze to the captain.

"Well, my people have some special areas of expertise. Phila may be able to patch something together. What about your wrist communicators? The *Jefferson* is within range—"

"They don't answer! We've been hailing till we're hoarse," said Serula angrily. "I know you can't approach a station without passing identification checks. But we're so crippled we can barely hold each other together."

"I think you ought to break up," said Kelly. "If they start firing, the whole squadron will go out in the chain reaction."

The admiral and Serula glanced at each other. After a slight hesitation, Serula gestured to her first officer and gave the order.

"Will they see our drifting apart as a hostile action?"

"If the science stations are doing their job," retorted Kelly, "they ought to know that you have neither weapons nor propulsion. You're no threat, and if they fire again they are in violation of—"

"Commander!" shouted Phila across the bridge, temporarily quieting the noise. "I've established a link with the *Jefferson.*"

"How?" began Serula in amazement, but Kelly was already hurrying across the bridge to crouch beside Phila.

She grinned at him. She was holding the circuit board on which had been rigged some kind of primitive Morse key. "The problem is that the system has been shorted out down to a few electric pulses. Not enough strength for voice transmissions, but enough for Morse, which is just dots and dashes anyway. Sconey is the communications officer on the *Jefferson.* Years ago, in Fleet training, we learned old Morse and used a bulkhead tap to send messages on the grapevine that the regular electronic snoops couldn't catch. I figure if I send Morse, and remind him that he owes me fifty credits, he'll know we aren't aliens."

Nothing could beat the noncom network of favors and debts. Relieved, Kelly squeezed her shoulder. "Good thinking! You just earned your pay for the week."

Her dark eyes gleamed. "How about a raise?"

"Captain, they've stopped. They're just sitting out there," said someone.

A babble of relieved voices broke out.

"That will do!" said Serula sharply, restoring order. She joined Kelly and frowned down at the sending key as though she hadn't a clue as to what it was. "They are looking us over. Have they replied?"

"Not officially," said Phila. "Just a recognition from Sconey. Uh, he's the *Jefferson's* comm officer. Something coming in now."

They all waited, tense, until Phila finished translating. Then she looked up with a grin. "Message reads: *Jefferson* to *Sounder*. Apologies for firing. Permission to send over a boarding party."

A cheer went up. Serula's shoulders sagged a bit. She smiled at Phila. "My compliments to Captain Lewis. Permission granted."

As Phila went to work, Serula glanced at Kelly. "Would you care to greet them aboard, Commander?"

It was a polite way of giving him the chance to rub in Lewis' faulty judgment. But Kelly didn't need the satisfaction of saying I told you so. He shook his head and looked right at his father.

"I would rather," he said, "know who shot you to pieces like this."

"That's classified," said the admiral promptly.

As stubborn as the admiral suddenly looked, Kelly felt even more determined to have some answers. Touching his father's elbow, he led the admiral over to a quiet corner.

"Dad, can the classified bit," he said in a low voice. "My clearance is high enough. You've come out of Nielson's Void and whatever happened, it was big enough to knock around a whole squadron. Plus," he added before his father could interrupt, "squadrons have five destroyers, not six. Which tells me that number six is part of a second squadron. What happened to it? Is it back in the Void, even more disabled than this one?"

The admiral's lean face looked suddenly old and tired. He rubbed his eyes, and the weariness in that small gesture awoke Kelly's compassion. But he said nothing, waiting for his father to answer.

"No, Blue Squadron is not back there," he said at last, his voice so low Kelly had to strain to hear it. "The *Sounder* was my observer ship in Blue Squadron. We had engine trouble and had to pull out of maneuvers. And then, right in the middle of the action, Blue Squadron disappeared."

It took Kelly a moment to register what the admiral had said. "Disappeared? I don't understand."

"Vanished. One moment out there. The next moment . . . *gone.*" The admiral shook his head. "Some kind of anomaly, a rip in the fabric of space itself."

"Big enough to swallow four destroyers?" asked Kelly. "I know there are a few points of space interphasing. At least that's the theory scientists postulate to explain what they are. Small ships can slip through although usually you have enough instrument trouble to warn you before you get too close—"

"No warning," snapped the admiral. "No propulsion drift. No excessive course corrections. No distortions registered beforehand. They all faded at the same time. Afterward, there was excessive disturbance."

"Enough to cause all this damage?"

"No." The admiral's voice cracked and he swallowed, clenching his fists. "No, something came through that hole. It's a door between universes perhaps. Or perhaps it's a door between times. Maybe it's a wormhole, although no one could find any evidence of a collapsed star in the vicinity. My God." The admiral buried his face in his hands a moment.

Frowning, Kelly gently put his hand on the admiral's shoulder. "You need to sit down somewhere. You're exhausted."

The admiral snapped erect, shaking off Kelly's solicitation almost angrily. "Don't coddle me! They came through and wiped us out in minutes. Our weapons couldn't compete. I don't think we pierced their shielding a single time. Then they were gone. I don't know who they are or where they come from. But if they have opened a door and if they plan to come out again, we've already shown them that they won't encounter much resistance."

"Plus they've got four of our ships," said Kelly. "What kind of vessels do they have? Did they attempt any communications with you before they opened fire?"

"No more than Captain Lewis," said the admiral bitterly. "I can't give you specifics. The log recordings can show you what happened. I have copies sealed for delivery to Commodore West. Jedderson ought to see them, but he's too far away, and we need to take action now. All I know is that I felt a crushing sense of malevolence. That's neither scientific nor logical. But I felt it. Whoever they are, they aren't our friends."

Kelly thought it over a moment, considering the implications of what might prove to be the exploratory tip of an invasion force.

"You have my squad," he said. "I have full crew complement. Just no ship and no equipment. We're at your disposal, no matter what West says."

The admiral smiled briefly. "Still not getting along with West? You always did have trouble with authority. But I think you can be useful. We'll need specialists when we go back."

"Now wait a minute," said Kelly in surprise. "I was just kidding. You aren't planning to turn around and go straight back out there, are you?"

"Yes, I am."

"Dad," said Kelly, trying to clear that grim look from his father's face. "Your ship can barely crawl. You can't—"

The famous Kelly glare pinned him to the wall. "I intend to confiscate the *Jefferson* for investigative purposes," said the admiral. "This isn't a matter for bureaucratic debate. Someone has breached our galaxy, Bryan, and it's up to us to plug that hole."

"Dad—"

But the admiral was turning away. "Ah, here comes the boarding party from the *Jefferson*. Junior officers still wet behind the ears from the looks of them. Minus their captain." He snorted. "All expendables. I'm surprised he didn't send over a couple of repair drones just to be extra safe."

Kelly remained silent. He knew that tone of his father's. It didn't bode well for Captain Lewis. But the admiral was going to have to stand in line when it came to dealing with one obstinate, bull-headed dimwit of a career officer.

"Bryan?"

"Yes, sir?"

The admiral looked at him in appeal. "I need you on this. You aren't in the Fleet, so I can't give you a direct order.

You've already risked your life, your crew, and your ship for me today. But I need your expertise and your support."

Kelly studied him a moment. He couldn't remember when his father had ever needed him. Loved him, yes. Always. But needed him? In spite of the strong feeling that he needed to know more about this situation before he let himself get mixed up in it, Kelly let a slow grin spread across his face.

"In case you have to take the *Jefferson* by force?" he asked.

The admiral stiffened. "I have the authority to commandeer any ship to my flag in an emergency. I won't be hijacking her."

"Oh, yes, you are," said Kelly, and held out his hand. "Count the Hawks in."

3

The conference room of the *Jefferson* lacked enough chairs; its temperature thermostats were failing to kick on at a decent cycle, making the room too hot; and the science officer's monotone made concentration difficult.

"After exhaustive analysis of the log recordings, we have been able to determine power utilization curves of the alien vessels. Our findings indicate that they—"

"We'll worry later about how fast they can go," interrupted the admiral. "I want to know where they came from."

The science officer sighed and shifted her gaze to Captain Lewis. The captain, however, sat glumly in his chair and glowered at the far wall. As well he should, for men with better track records than his had found themselves out of a job for lesser mistakes. The admiral had come aboard the *Jefferson* in dress uniform, medals blazing upon his chest, and was escorted by a full complement of adjutants. There had already been a formal ceremony of transferring the admiral's flag to the *Jefferson*. Lewis had made no protest.

He hadn't a leg to stand on, and he was experienced enough to know it.

Thus far the admiral had not spoken to Lewis any more than was necessary. He had not referred once to the fact that Lewis had nearly destroyed the helpless squadron or had nearly killed his son and his son's crew. There had been a long moment when the two men stared at each other. The admiral's blue eyes had been like ice, and Lewis had looked away first. Lewis' own conscience could twist him harder than any reprimand.

"Well?" repeated the admiral. His cultured, well-modulated voice sharped only a fraction, but it was enough to make the science officer flinch. "Any theories?"

"Yes, sir. We first considered the idea of an invisibility device, due primarily to the fact that you encountered no anomalies prior to Blue Squadron's disappearance. But our physics is not advanced enough to find a solution to the problem of the tremendous amount of energy necessary to render a whole squadron invisible.

"That leaves us with the idea of a parallel universe."

"And an interstitial interphase. Yes," said the admiral. He glanced at his son, and Kelly raised his eyebrows. Kelly hated conferences. He preferred to do his theorizing on the way to the action. "But it seems an erratic way of opening a door to an invasion."

"They may not be planning an invasion," said the science officer. "It could have been purely a reactionary move. They were startled by Blue Squadron's passage through the door, and they—"

"Don't speculate where you aren't called upon to do so," said the admiral.

The science officer turned red. There fell a moment of silence.

Kelly leaned his elbows upon the table, which was marred by old coffee rings and worn, discolored patches. "As I understand it, interphasing is erratic," he said. "Could they have—"

"Interphasing is only one means of contact between parallel universes," said the science officer, recovering her composure. "The more accepted theory is derived from maximal geometry, in which for every Schwarzschild black hole there is a counterpart on the other side called a white hole."

"Ah," said the admiral. "We considered wormholes, at least until those devils came swarming out of nowhere. But not white holes."

"That won't work," said Kelly. "We could go in through a black hole, but they wouldn't be able to come out at the same point. If I remember my old physics course correctly, matter can't enter a white hole. That would mean they have to have a nearby black hole on their side in order to come into our universe."

"Well, there wasn't a black hole there," said the admiral shortly. "As for a white hole, I wouldn't know one if I ran into it."

Lewis snorted to himself as though he could bear to keep quite no longer. "Mathematical poppycock," he rumbled. "Nothing proven."

The science officer looked more nervous than ever. Kelly felt sorry for her, caught between the admiral and Lewis.

"There is also the possibility of time travel," she said. Everyone looked at her, and her gaze shifted about rapidly to avoid contact with anyone. "Of course that requires a rotating black hole. With two horizons, the space between becomes time. With each interchange, or the point of intersection between space and time—"

Lewis snorted even louder.

"Well," faltered the science officer. "As I said, these are only theories."

"Yes, and next you will have us traveling to negative space." Lewis spun his chair about and slapped the conference table with his palm. "Or playing with closed time loops. Poppycock, all of it! The admiral has stated there are no black holes in the vicinity. I can't imagine maneuvers being carried out near one in any case."

"Unless," said Kelly softly, watching his father's hands, which were resting lightly upon the table, "for some classified reason that we haven't been told, there is a manufactured black hole in Nielson's Void for the purpose of—"

The admiral's left hand twitched. "Don't go off into fantasy," he said with irritation. "Two centuries ago, we figured out that it was not economically feasible to make stellar-mass collapsars."

"But not miniature ones," said Kelly. "How about it? Has someone on the other side opened a gate into our universe, or is the Fleet busy punching holes—"

"No!" said Captain Serula, jumping to her feet. Until now she had been silent, sitting out of Kelly's line of vision. She still wore her crumpled uniform. She had the white, glassy look of someone operating beyond exhaustion. "We were testing weapons, not trying to enter another dimension. And why can't we do something about what's happened instead of just sitting here talking about it? Why aren't we going after them, trying to help them?"

"We will," said Kelly. He had meant to goad his father, not this officer who must be feeling the unjustified, but understandable guilt of having been spared Blue Squadron's fate by a fluke engine malfunction. "But we need to know what we're up against first."

She blinked, and the fierceness faded from her face. In silence she sank back into her chair. Kelly glanced around to find his father glaring at him. Kelly gave him a slight shrug of apology.

"If it is an invasion force," said the admiral. "We must stop it at the source."

"And if this is just the first gateway?" asked Kelly.

"Then we close it, and all the others." The admiral stood up. "I want these disabled ships assisted back to Station 4. I want a direct transmission to Fleet HQ. And I want this kept bottled. No public discussion of it on Station 4 by anyone, at any level. If I know Jedderson, he'll send out all the forces at his disposal. But in the meantime someone has to guard that area."

Lewis rose slowly to his feet. Craggy and stocky in build, he had to look up to meet the admiral's eyes. "I assume that the *Jefferson* is being assigned the job?"

"That's right."

Lewis pulled in his chin, making his jowls fold over his collar. "We are not at full power. We were in for repairs after that skirmish on the Salukan border. We aren't—"

"You can move and you can fight. The ship will do," said the admiral.

"Sir, I respectfully protest what I feel to be—"

"You feel to be what!" roared the admiral. "An unfair assignment? Scut duty? I don't see guarding our galaxy from invasion as the bottom of a desirable action list. Need I add cowardice to your faults, sir?"

Lewis turned a dark shade of crimson. "I can answer that accusation at your convenience, Admiral!"

Kelly got to his feet, as did the others in the room. Consternation could be seen on every face. First Officer Jordan stepped up to Lewis.

"Sir," he said worriedly. "You can't challenge a superior officer to a duel. Regulations specifically forbid—"

"And etiquette is even stricter on that point," put in one of the admiral's better-tailored adjutants. "No officer may respond to a reprimand with a challenge."

Lewis clenched his fists. "You don't have to spout the rule book at me! I know the damned thing perfectly well."

"Then you know that you are out of order, sir," said the admiral sharply. "I am relieving you of the command which you show yourself unfit for. You may transfer your belongings to the ESS *Dragon* by 1430 hours. That's fifteen minutes from now."

"You can't do that! You can't take my ship! By God, I'll have you charged for this. You and that oddball son of yours think you own the Fleet, think you can do as you please, run over whom you please, and never mind those of us who came up through the ranks the hard way. You'll—"

The admiral made a small gesture, and Captain Lewis was cleared from the room, still shouting.

The quiet left behind was a relief. Kelly circled the table and came to stand beside the admiral.

"You handled that neatly," he said, his voice carefully neutral. "Made him finish himself off. He'll probably have to take a medical leave. He probably will never command a ship again."

The admiral's eyes flashed. "Medical leave, my foot. I'm having him charged with attempted murder."

Kelly put out his hand. "Don't."

"Why not?" Then the admiral's fierceness cooled slightly. "Because of you? Damn it, Bryan, the fact that you're my son has nothing to do with that man's incompetence. He destroyed a proto-class cruiser. There aren't too many of those around. Now, don't be a soft fool."

Kelly stepped back, suddenly conscious that Captain Serula had remained in the room to witness this conversation. He glanced at her, but she didn't appear to even be listening. Her face was pensive and tight with grief.

The admiral followed Kelly's glance and his own expression softened. "Captain Serula," he said with a gentleness that surprised Kelly. "I'm putting you in command of this ship. We'll be setting course immediately for Nielson's Void. Would you give the necessary orders, please?"

Serula looked at him as though coming back from far away. A smile lit in the depths of her gray eyes and slowly spread to the rest of her face. "Yes, sir. Thank you."

The admiral smiled back. "If you want any specific crew members from the *Sounder* or any of the other ships in Red Squadron, have them come over at once. We need the best we've got."

Serula nodded and started out.

"One other thing," said the admiral after her.

"Sir?"

"Get some rest. Consider that a direct order."

She left, and Kelly faced his father.

"Is Serula up to this? She looks pretty shaky to me."

"Nonsense. She's a seasoned officer, as tough a commander as they come. She'll bear up."

Kelly had his doubts, but his father's tone left no room for further discussion. Excusing himself, Kelly headed out into the corridor, took a few wrong turns, and finally managed to cross paths with Captain Lewis, on his way to the teleport bay. A young yeoman struggled to carry the captain's gear, and Lewis walked alone, avoided by the gazes of his crew as he passed them in the corridor.

"Captain Lewis!"

At Kelly's shout Lewis dragged his slumping shoulders erect and turned like an old bear at bay. He waited until Kelly caught up with him. At close range, his small eyes glittered.

"Come to rub it in?" he said gruffly. "How many officers have you broken between the two of you? I remember Commodore Santini, one of the finest men who ever lived. We were at Academy together. You mutinied, turned his crew against him, and ruined him in the last years of his career."

The attack hit home. Kelly frowned to hide it, but Lewis had seen. He bared his teeth.

"I stood at court-martial," said Kelly defensively. Inside he felt the old weariness. Would he never stop defending his actions in the Battle of Capellstran? Would he never stop paying for having been right? "I was exonerated of all charges. Santini wasn't. The investigations were thorough."

"They were rigged," said Lewis. "All the old-line officers knew it. That's why you dropped out of the service after your trial. You knew what would happen to you under another commander."

"That's untrue—"

"Oh, I know all about these old Fleet families. Generation after generation of service. The admiral thinks he's God and you and your brother expect to inherit the universe after him."

White heat flashed in Kelly's face. For a moment he could hear nothing at all. His fists came up and in an instant he had Lewis pinned against the wall.

But the taunting satisfaction in Lewis' face dashed cold reason over Kelly. If the captain could get him to strike him, that would undermine the admiral's charges against Lewis and give the old captain a foothold back into the service. Kelly stepped back, breathing heavily in an effort to master his temper.

"It won't work, Lewis," he said. "We haven't gotten where we are because of special favors or family reputation. You can brood on class differences all day long, but that doesn't make them a reality. You made the mistake today. I didn't. That's all there is to it. I'm sorry you didn't listen."

"Go to hell!" said Lewis viciously, and shouldered past him.

Kelly watched him disappear around the curve of the corridor. Only then did he lean against the wall and wipe the perspiration from his palms. He still felt unsteady with anger that burned hot under his rib cage. The old prejudices from the first days of the Fleet had never been eradicated. Up-through-the-ranks officers versus Academy officers. Experience versus training. It wasn't supposed to be like that, yet it seemed to get worse, to become more bitter, every year.

With a sigh Kelly went off to find his squad.

Looking odd in their civilian clothes, they'd collected in a rec room, where all of the game equipment looked as though it had been disconnected. The air had the stale, too-often-recycled smell of old compressors. Kelly realized for the first time that the *Valiant* was truly gone, and her newness and beauty with her. His home . . . and theirs.

His gaze swept their faces, then he abruptly turned away and dropped into a chair.

Caesar approached him. "Have some coffee, boss. It tastes like heated bilge, but there's nothing like raw caffeine to put you on the edge."

Kelly took the cup. "Thanks."

Except for 41 and Ouoji, who prowled the farthest perimeters of the room like a pair exploring their cage, everyone huddled close to one another in a seating U around a blank game table. The *Valiant* had been their reference point. Now they looked at Kelly, lost, as though he was all they had left.

"Something wrong, Commander?" asked Beaulieu.

His head came up at the clinical question. "Not beyond the obvious."

"Did you get that *cosquenti* Lewis?" asked Phila angrily. "How long do we have to stay on his ship?"

"It's not his ship any longer. Captain Serula has been placed in charge, and Lewis is on his way back to Station 4."

Caesar tipped back his head. "There is justice in this galaxy!"

"Good going, Commander!"

"I didn't do it," said Kelly sharply, putting his untasted coffee aside. "The admiral tossed him."

Phila grinned. "Your daddy. Same difference."

Anger flashed through Kelly, but he curbed it hard. This wasn't the time to lose his temper. Still, Caesar saw it and elbowed Phila to be quiet.

"So what happens now?" asked Siggerson quietly. "Do we return to the station? West isn't going to be happy with us, leaving without authority and getting the *Valiant* blown to bits."

His voice as he spoke was level and controlled, but his eyes were hard with reproach and blame.

"No, we're under mission now," said Kelly, deciding this was as good a time as any to tell them. "The admiral has asked us to assist him."

"What's cooking, boss? I smell fish," said Caesar.

Kelly told them all that he knew. While he was talking 41 wandered back to join the group, standing slightly apart. When Kelly finished, 41 was the first to speak.

"They sound like the Invaders. The Old Ones who raised me spoke of them. But they were said to have been destroyed by the Svetzin."

"The Svetzin!" said Siggerson in surprise. "That race was extinct at least a thousand years ago."

41 shrugged. "The Old Ones had long memories. Is there a tape of these who attacked?"

"Just of their ships," said Kelly in curiosity. The odd quirks of 41's past never failed to amaze him. He pointed at the viewer, and 41 crossed the room to activate it. Kelly had to clear 41's request, and then they were all crowding around to watch the tape. By now heartily tired of watching the battle, the disappearance of the four ships, and the sudden appearance of nine black-hulled marauders, Kelly leveled his attention upon 41's lean, bronzed face, watching it for any hint of recognition.

But as usual, 41's expression gave little away of what he was thinking. He watched with total concentration, seemingly oblivious to the others' comments, and when the tape ended he requested a second run-through.

"Well?" said Kelly at last.

41's tawny eyes met his. "They are the same. The pattern of attack and the black-hulled ships. These are old tales that I heard many times, of their coming into the skies as locusts, engulfing a world and slaying all upon it, only to depart as rapidly as they came. It was said they searched for a world to make their own. Yet none ever satisfied. They could not be frightened for death meant nothing to them. Life meant less. They showed no mercy to those they vanquished. They took Saulis, Amazeran, Koth—"

"Koth!" said Beaulieu, frowning. "But these are mythical civilizations, legends never proven."

"They flourished until the coming of the Invaders," said 41. "Then they were no more. The Svetzin arose and pulled together the mightiest fleet of their long history. They sought out the Invaders and attacked them. They journeyed to the gateway and found it as this tape shows, a shimmer in the void, nothing seen and therefore unable to be closed. The Invaders fought like the ten furies of Halsbane, and yet the Svetzin had taken an oath to defeat them, unto the last drop of Svetzin blood."

41's eyes flashed fiercely. "It did take it. But they defeated the Invaders. And the last Svetzin ship journeyed through the gate that was not there, never to return. Thus it was closed for all time."

"Until now," said Kelly softly.

The others looked at him.

"Maybe," said Beaulieu.

Phila's dark eyes glowed over the tale. Siggerson frowned in skepticism. Caesar made a face and wandered away, shaking his head. Beaulieu stared at 41 with a thoughtful look as though she wanted to dissect him.

"Sounds pretty similar to me," said Kelly. "What if they are the same people? What if they've opened another gate, and intend to come through again?"

"But that's nonsense," said Siggerson. "Why wait a thousand years? If they had the capability then, it wouldn't have been lost—"

"It might have been. The Svetzin might have defeated them enough to set them back a long time."

"No civilization holds the same goal that long."

"None in our experience," said Kelly. "We don't know what we're up against. The admiral said he felt a malevolence. He's not prone to flights of fancy or even hunches. For him to admit something like that, it must have been a pretty strong feeling."

"An old ghost story and you're going to believe it?" asked Siggerson, looking from Kelly to 41. "I suppose next you'll decide that we should go through that anomaly after the missing ships—"

"Why not?" said Kelly. They started to protest and he put

up his hands. "Hear me out. It's our job to perform tasks the Fleet can't. Investigation and rescue, remember? We have to know what's become of those four ships. If possible, we have to get them and their crews back."

"They could be dead by now, smeared four millimeters thick on the surface of some rock," said Siggerson in impatience.

"Then we'll confirm it," said Kelly. "That's the job, people."

"We don't have orders from West," said Siggerson. "Who's decided this is our job? You?"

"That's right," said Kelly levelly. "The admiral asked for our help, and I've offered it."

"The admiral," said Siggerson despite Caesar's warning tug on his sleeve, "sounds like he's gone overboard on this invasion of the galaxy theory. He spooked when the ships winked out—"

"Wouldn't you?" asked Caesar hotly. "Go stiff yourself, Siggerson. You're just mad because we trashed the *Valiant* to save a few hundred lives. Pull together or ship out."

Siggerson's eyes were like charcoal in the white stretch of his face. "Ship out," he said, nodding. "Not such a bad idea. I don't know how I ever got roped into this outfit in the first place."

Turning on his heel he strode away, calling to Ouoji as he went.

41 spoke at Kelly's shoulder: "Do I stop him?"

Kelly shook his head. "It has to be free choice or nothing."

"Good riddance," said Caesar. "He never was a Hawk anyway. Nothing but a computer brain with a polarized nodule for a heart. Pilots are easy to replace."

Phila shrugged and said nothing. Beaulieu, however, frowned after Siggerson as though she wanted to do or say something to bring him back.

Siggerson paused at the door and glanced over his shoulder. "Ouoji! Come here."

Ouoji, who'd been sniffing delicately beneath a chair, now bounced out into the open. But instead of running after him, she sat down and wrapped her long, fluffy tail tightly around her feet. Her blue eyes slitted in disapproval.

"Ouoji, I'm going back to Station 4. If we don't leave now, we'll have to go on this cockeyed mission. So come along."

Ouoji's furry ear flaps lifted, then clamped tightly shut again. She made no other move.

After a moment Siggerson snorted. "I guess you've got some notion that you have to stay with the *Valiant*. Only there isn't one anymore. Your duty is off. Understand?"

Ouoji flipped the tip of her tail to indicate that she did understand, but she did not move.

Hurt showed briefly in Siggerson's face before anger replaced it. "Fine," he said, and started out the door.

Ouoji leapt forward, dashing past Siggerson to cut him off. She faced him, coming only to knee height, but looking larger than usual with her fur fuzzed out. Her tail lashed from side to side, and she chittered long and angrily.

"She's telling him," said Caesar. "Go to it, Ouoji!"

Siggerson stood there until Ouoji paused, then he said, "This is absurd." He started to step around her, but she wrapped her tail about his ankle and darted between his legs with a stout yank that toppled him off balance.

He went sprawling onto his backside. Before he could scramble up, Ouoji jumped onto his stomach and put her face in his, chittering more vehemently than ever.

Kelly exchanged looks with the others and started to smile.

"You'd better rescue him, boss," said Caesar. "The last time I tried to pet her when she was all riled up, she bit my finger."

Kelly went to the pilot. "Ouoji," he said quietly. "Hey, Ouoji, lighten up. I think Siggerson gets the message."

She ignored him and continued her tirade for several minutes, finishing with a series of little growls and a bump of her round head under Siggerson's chin as though to show there were no permanent hard feelings.

At this point 41 scooped her up. She bounded to his shoulder and curled around his head to peer at Siggerson. Kelly touched Siggerson's chest to hold him in place.

"Are you staying on the team?" he asked. He tried not to laugh openly, but the corners of his mouth kept curling.

Siggerson looked from him to Ouoji and back again. He grimaced. "I seem to have no choice. Commander Ouoji has spoken."

Kelly laughed and gave him a hand up. "Good. We need you. I won't deny that. And when this is finished, we'll get another ship."

Siggerson shrugged and said nothing.

Phila activated the viewer and the screen showed the other ships pulling away. "It's too late anyway," she said. "Like it or not, we're stuck with this job now."

"One starship against 41's race of Invaders," said Caesar mournfully. "Do you think this hulk has a bar? I need a stiff drink."

4

Kelly had been in Nielson's Void only once before, and that was long ago during his time as an ensign. Three days later the *Jefferson* slowed from TD 4 and flashed her security codes at the warning buoys. At a cautious sublight pace she entered the zone that was forbidden to all civilian spacecraft.

The main viewscreen on the narrow, equipment-crammed bridge showed very few stars, like a dim scattering of dust far away. On a whim the science officer was playing engine rumble over audio, giving them the illusion of listening to themselves against the infinite silence of space.

The void was truly empty. No asteroid belts, no nebulae, no cinderball remnants of planets spinning on a rogue course, no comets, no dust clouds, no young stars or old stars . . . nothing to get in the way of whatever testing the military wanted to conduct. They didn't even have the spectacular spectrum band of color caused by bending light waves to watch now that they were going at sublight.

Kelly stood and gazed into the darkness, feeling it suck at

his vision. It was said that sailors of old used to become mesmerized by the wake of their vessels upon Earth's seas until they fell overboard to their deaths. He had always found the glitter of stars and planets to be hypnotic. Now, their absence disturbed him. He shifted on his feet, frowning.

Ship's sensors were scanning on maximum sweep. Nothing had registered. They were utterly, completely alone, a speck of dust in the cosmos. Vulnerable and tiny in the pressurized protection of a pyrillium hull with a few plasma cannons against whatever waited for them to venture closer.

A hand touched Kelly's shoulder. "Commander?"

He jumped and spun around, already feeling the swift heat of embarrassment. He found himself looking into the gray eyes of Captain Serula.

"Sorry," he said sheepishly. "I was letting my fancies run away with me."

Serula smiled. Her skin had lost its pallor. She looked more rested, but no less haunted. "The Void is one creepy sector of space. We're almost to the coordinates where Blue Squadron disappeared. I've decided to launch both shuttle-craft. Your squad will be in one, and a science team will be in the other."

Kelly didn't like the idea and started to say so, but Serula raised her brows coolly at him.

"Triangulation," she said. "We might as well spread our meager forces as far as we can. By the way, I'm coming with you."

"Oh, no, you're not," said Kelly before he could stop himself.

Engine rumble quieted on the speakers, and conversations upon the bridge died down as the duty crew got ready to listen. Serula drew in an audible breath and snapped him a look of exasperation.

"There will be no discussion," she said curtly. "Prepare for launch in thirty minutes. Shuttlebay 2."

Thus dismissed from the bridge, Kelly had no choice but

to leave and get to work. His squad, finally in uniform, was ready, but there were last-minute checks to run as they loaded their gear upon the shuttle. It was a cramped craft, shaped like a crescent, with the propulsion jets centered on the inside curve. Siggerson wedged his lanky body into the pilot's seat where there wasn't room for his long legs and scowled at the instrumentation. Ouoji perched on his shoulder, studying the controls with visible interest.

"A child could fly this," said Siggerson. "It's designed for the simplest possible operation."

"Then why don't you put Ouoji in the driver's seat?" said Caesar, tossing another gear bag to Phila, who was loading compartments in the left wing.

Ouoji turned her round head and squinted at Caesar in amusement. She patted Siggerson where his hair was balding on the crown as though to remind him to keep his temper.

"Look sharp," said Kelly. "Serula wants to go with us."

They stopped work at once.

"Why?"

"We don't need her in the way."

"Boss—"

Kelly raised his hands. "Agreed. We don't need her. She's like a time bomb, waiting to detonate."

"Stress," said Beaulieu, still counting off things on her checklist. "Compounded by the fact that her husband was commanding one of the ships that vanished out here."

Even Kelly hadn't known that. He dropped his duffel onto a seat and stared at Beaulieu. "How did you find that out?"

She shrugged. "Simple. I read the medical logs. The admiral's decision to let her command the *Jefferson* back out here is one thing. Her going along with us is another—"

"Right," said Kelly. "She isn't going. Finish this up. We're planning an early launch."

"No, you're not," said Serula's voice. Her lilting accent

was almost lost in the grim flatness of her tone. She stood at the open hatch of the shuttle, looking in at them.

Kelly wondered how much she had overheard. The anger in her gaze told him she had heard everything. He faced her without apology.

"Okay, Captain. We couldn't slug it out on the bridge in front of your crew. But this is my crew. They are highly trained specialists. They work precisely together. You aren't needed. You will be in the way."

"I can handle more than a starship," she said. "And I don't have to ask your permission to come along."

She stepped into the shuttle, but 41 blocked her path. She glared at him, but he didn't budge.

"Get out of my way, operative," she snapped. "That's an order."

41 bared his teeth.

Serula blinked and took a second look at him. She drew back slightly. "Commander, call this man aside."

"He's following my orders," said Kelly, "and we don't follow yours. Go back to your bridge, Captain."

She flushed. "I can't do anything there. Look, Kelly. I'm not trying to take charge. I just want to be a part of the rescue. I overheard you talking to the admiral. I know that you intend to go through the gateway if you can find it." She frowned. "Not many would try something like that. I—I appreciate it, and I want to help."

"Stay with the *Jefferson*," said Kelly more gently. "That's where your abilities lie. We'll do our best to bring back your husband, and the others."

"I can't stay here!" she said. "The admiral can command this ship. I can't just pace the bridge, waiting, doing nothing. Don't you understand? I should have gone through the gateway with the others. I was the team leader, not Richard. I—"

"You may need to exorcise your own sense of guilt, but that's not my responsibility," said Kelly.

She flinched, and he was sorry he had to be so harsh.

Behind him, Siggerson said, "Five minutes to depressurization."

Kelly caught 41's eye. "Close the hatch. I'm sorry, Captain."

He turned away from her frustrated face. 41 hit the closure control and reached up to guide the slowly descending hatch. Serula tried to climb in under it, but 41 shoved her back.

Shaking his head, Kelly climbed into his seat and began strapping in. The low whine of the closing hatch stopped. He glanced up, saw it only half closed, and frowned.

"41? What are you—"

Without looking at him, 41 hit the top control and the hatch lifted. Then 41 stepped back, his back rigid, his hands held quietly at his sides.

"Hey!" said Caesar, but Kelly gestured tensely for silence.

Serula entered with a small bi-muzzled pistol aimed at 41's midsection. The expression in her gray eyes gave no doubt at all that she would use it if necessary.

Fuming, Kelly sat there along with the others and made no move as 41 continued to back into the seating area. When his back was pressed against Beaulieu's seat, Serula hit the closure control. The hatch dropped smoothly. It muffled the humming vibration of the small engines.

Siggerson glanced at her and dropped his hands in his lap. Without glancing at him, Serula said, "As you were, pilot. Fly us out of here nice and easy or I'm going to take all my frustration out on this man."

"This is stupid, Serula," began Kelly. "You can't—"

Her gaze shifted to Kelly, and 41 made his move. Serula shot 41, sending him reeling against the wall with a grunt of pain.

The recoil of the plasma weapon screamed in the small enclosed space. Kelly bolted up, but Serula trained her weapon on him. He froze. Behind him, Caesar and Phila were poised, just waiting for a chance to take her. Kelly glanced at 41, who was doubled over against the wall, making little sounds of agony.

"41?"

"He's just stunned," said Serula. "But I don't have to be that nice." Her fingers shifted on the pistol and Kelly heard the low whine of a lethal charge.

His breath tangled up in his throat. He glanced again at 41, thankful the operative wasn't really hurt although stuns at such point-blank range could be serious enough. In the wake of his relief came scalding fury.

"Are you crazy!" he shouted. "What the hell do you think you're doing, shooting up my squad just to get your way?"

The comm began beeping, distracting him. Siggerson reached for it, only to freeze as Serula's pistol leveled itself centimeters from his right ear. His throat worked as he swallowed. Then he touched the control and replied.

"Attention, shuttlecraft," said the admiral's voice. "If Captain Serula is down there to send you off, tell her she's needed on the bridge."

"Yes, sir," said Siggerson in an absolutely neutral voice.

"One other thing," said the admiral. "What is your usual send off? Safe flight and home again?"

"That is correct," said Siggerson. "Thank you."

He broke the line.

The pistol swung to a neutral position where Serula could cover him, 41, and Kelly.

"Everyone, take your seats," she said.

The shuttle began turning on its landing platform, pivoting into launch position. Kelly eased around Beaulieu's seat and went to 41's assistance. 41 still could not straighten fully. He leaned on Kelly, his jaw clenched so hard the muscles bulged. Kelly felt sorry for him. He knew all too well the effects: the miserable, aching nausea that could not be relieved, the cold sweats, the dizzying sensation of not being able to breathe.

A flash of 41's golden eyes beneath the tangle of his hair

betrayed a fury that didn't bode well for Serula in the future. 41 was capable of considerable patience, but when the time was right he would stalk and he would strike. Kelly knew he would have to intervene later, but at the moment he wanted to readjust Serula himself.

"Easy," he said quietly to 41, staggering along with most of 41's weight on him. "It'll wear off soon."

He maneuvered 41 past Beaulieu, who along with Caesar lent a hand to lower 41 into a seat and strap him in. His bronzed skin had turned a sickly shade of yellow, and perspiration beaded his temples. Beaulieu checked his pulse and his pupils, then ran her hand along his left shoulder and arm.

"Feel any of that?" she asked.

He half closed his eyes and gave the barest indication of a headshake. His breathing remained jerky. At that close range he was lucky his heart hadn't stopped.

"Good old Salukan stamina," said Beaulieu with a brief smile for 41 alone.

"Everyone, strap in," said Serula.

Phila had already taken her seat. She sat there glaring steadily at Serula with her fierce black eyes. Caesar, his usual clownish humor missing, took the place beside 41. Kelly reseated himself beside Beaulieu, and Serula slid into the copilot's seat, swiveling it where she could watch all of them.

When her gaze came to rest upon Kelly, he said, "You'd better hope he's recovered by the time we get out there."

"He will be," she said. "You're overreacting, Commander. We're in this together, all on the same side—"

"Don't count on it, toots," said Caesar in a soft, grim voice.

"Stand by for launch," said Siggerson.

The shuttlebay doors opened, and space yawned before them.

"Down their throat," said Kelly.

Siggerson touched the controls, and a green light began flashing rapidly over the bay doors.

"Launching . . . now."

The sling beneath them tipped them to a forty-five degree angle. Seconds later the boost thrust them forward with a shuddering, crushing g-force. The shuttle rumbled loudly, vibrating like crazy. Just as Kelly began to wonder if they were going to shake apart, the engine thrusters cut in, powering the stabilizers and smoothing out the ride rapidly.

By the time they had turned in a swift crescent away from the stern of the *Jefferson*, Siggerson had everything under control with his usual competence.

"Setting in coordinates now," he said. "Should be twenty-seven minutes at this speed."

Serula's tense posture relaxed fractionally. She lowered the pistol to her lap.

Kelly glanced at 41, who was regaining his normal color, then at Caesar. "How's he doing? Feeling space sick, 41?"

As he spoke he swept his hand across his middle, surreptitiously pressing the release of his safety harness. Caesar's, he noted, was already released. Caesar's eyes glowed an intense green. Kelly met his gaze, then glanced at Phila. His hand flicked an almost imperceptible signal to remain still. She frowned, but obeyed.

Before Kelly could move, however, the storage compartment beneath the instrumentation abruptly banged open, startling Serula. She jerked in her seat as a streak of gray fur came hurtling right at her, hissing viciously.

Kelly sprang at her from the opposite direction. She was half prepared for him and swung the pistol his way. But he twisted it from her grip and tossed it in a quick pass to Caesar.

"Damn you!" Serula swung her fist at Kelly, but he ducked and managed to pin her arms to her sides. She struggled, kicking like a street fighter.

"Hold it!" said Caesar, and put the bi-muzzle right in her face.

Serula grew still. Cautiously Kelly released her and stepped back. Serula's eyes were so dilated they looked black. Her color drained away, and suddenly she dropped into her seat with a stricken look.

On the floor Ouoji balanced on her haunches and tugged at Kelly's leg. He bent down to her level.

"As for you," he said affectionately, touching her on the end of her nose, where she liked it best. "I guess you saved the day. Thanks."

Ouoji turned about smugly and jumped into Siggerson's lap.

"And now," said Serula in a hollow voice. "You'll take me back, and that's the end of me. Over the edge, just like Lewis. Only I suppose in my case, medical leave is justified."

"You can't lean on that excuse," said Beaulieu from her place beside 41. She was checking his pulse rate again, but her eyes glowered at Serula. "I'm registered in psychoanalysis. You're not crackers, just spoiled."

"Easy, Beaulieu," said Kelly. He swung his gaze to Serula. "We're not taking you back. We're a little too busy at the moment to play ferry service."

Serula's tense expression relaxed. She sat up straighter. "I thought you'd see things my way—"

"Huh!" said Caesar, still holding the pistol trained on her. "I say we jettison her. Put her in a suit and let her play with her toes. The observation shuttle can pick her up."

"You wouldn't dare!"

But Kelly was smiling. "That, Caesar, is a very good idea. You and Phila see to it, if you please."

"No!" said Serula. "You can't do that to me! I'm a Fleet officer. That's—"

"Shut up, ma'am," said Caesar. "Step to the rear—"

"No. I won't. You'll have to stuff me in a suit by force and I warn you I'll—"

"Do as you're told," said Caesar, "or I'll stun you here and now."

Phila took Serula's arm. "You remember the first rule about space suits, don't you, ma'am? No puking. And what's the first thing you feel like when you're stunned?"

Serula glared at her. "I get the message."

"Yeah," said Phila. "So move to the rear and put on a suit."

Serula started to do as she was told.

"Kelly," said Siggerson in a tone that immediately caught Kelly's attention. "Something weird here. I'm getting a fluctuation on the—"

It was all the warning they had before the ship tumbled sideways, exactly as though a gigantic, invisible hand had swept her aside. Kelly went bouncing off deck and console with bruising force. He tried to grasp something to hang on to, but the shuttle was doing an end-over-end spin. Every time he lodged himself, the floor became the ceiling. There were cries of pain and fear around him. Something had happened to the lights. He couldn't see much beyond the dim glow along the instrumentation panel. But their velocity felt wrong, and the shuttle was groaning from a stress she wasn't designed to take.

He feared at any moment she would come apart and spill them out into the icy arms of space.

Siggerson had also lost his place at the instruments. He clambered past Kelly, striving to regain the controls, but was jolted aside. Kelly reached out and managed to grab the base of the pilot's chair. Clinging grimly to that, he levered himself up, grunting as he was slung about, and groped for the stabilizer assist.

The keypad burned his fingers. Nothing responded.

"Straighten her out, Kelly!" shouted Siggerson.

"Can't! She's fused." Kelly wedged his body between the chair and the console, trying to free both hands. Helm readings flashed rapidly. They were going way off course.

He realized the power drive was still functioning, though erratically. If he boosted the drive unit, that might straighten them out of this deadly spin. Cutting power would leave them spinning for an eternity, with no friction to ever slow them down until they rammed an asteroid a few million miles from nowhere.

Siggerson was shouting, but in the noise and confusion, Kelly couldn't make out what he was saying.

The shuttle was shaking badly now, her hull screaming with strain. They had minutes, perhaps only seconds, to come out of this. Kelly hesitated no longer. He hit boost, felt the shuttle try to respond, then falter.

"Come on," he urged it. "Come on. Come on!"

Slowly the power drive cramped and sputtered and finally engaged. They flipped so violently Kelly was thrown clear across the width of the shuttle and slammed into a bulkhead. Blackness washed over his eyeballs. For a moment he was witless, too stunned to know what was happening. He kept trying to keep conscious, to move, to *think*, but his head seemed to have swelled double its usual size and things kept vagueing out on him.

A stab of pain through the side of his skull broke through his haze. He put his hand to it, felt blood stick to his fingers, and opened his eyes.

The lights were flickering on and off, giving him nightmarish impressions of what was happening. The shuttle seemed right side up again, if slightly canted. Siggerson or someone was at the controls. Bodies picked themselves up with groans. A babble of voices broke out. He winced, concerned because his vision seemed to be going.

"Kelly!"

Hands seized him, jolting him hard enough to make him grunt in pain. He blinked, couldn't quite see, realized that was because one eye was gummed shut, and peered uncertainly at 41 who was now crouched beside him.

Kelly stirred, but 41 held him in place.

"Don't move. Beaulieu is out cold. I will help you."

"Is she all right? What about the others? What about the shuttle? Where—"

"Wait." Again 41 held him still. "Count to five."

Kelly's head was still swimming. Vast irritation filled him, however. "For God's sake. I've got to know what is—"

"Count to five. Count to three."

"One. Two. Uh . . . three." Kelly grimaced. His head felt like a crushed melon. Dimly he was aware that if he didn't pass, 41 would never let him up. "Uh . . . three. Four." He felt sweaty, cold. "Five."

"What is your name?"

"K-Kelly." Exasperated, Kelly thrust 41 back and squirmed past him, faltering, then using 41's shoulder as a lever to push himself up. "I'm all right," he said, swaying.

41 surged up beside him and grabbed his arm, but it was just to steady him. Kelly looked around, saw Phila bending over Beaulieu's unconscious form, saw Caesar speaking to Siggerson, didn't see Serula or Ouoji. He squinted. The flickering lights were giving him a headache.

"Can't we get these lights to steady?" he said. He wiped some of the blood from his face and staggered over to Siggerson.

"That's a big negative, boss," said Caesar cheerfully. His green eyes, however, held concern as they studied Kelly. "We're lucky we still got air."

"Sig?" asked Kelly. He didn't like nicknames and he'd meant to say Siggerson's full name, but somehow all of it never came out that time.

Siggerson didn't seem to notice. Without looking up, he said, "I'm trying to bring us around. Our steering's shot to hell. The stabilizers are gone. I can handle us on full manual for a while, but without the computer compensating, we'll start shaking soon. This crate is fragile, not intended to take any sort of pounding."

"And not Minzanese made, I'll bet," said Caesar. "What a loop we made, eh, boss? I think I left my stomach back there somewhere. What did you run us into anyway, Siggie? One minute we're fine; the next, we're slammed. Like getting whacked out of the way."

"Or knocked aside while a gate opened," said 41.

Kelly forced himself to concentrate. "That's it. That's what happened. The gateway opened. But we didn't go through."

"Nonsense," said Siggerson sharply. "We hadn't reached the coordinates yet."

"Who says the gate has to always be in the same place?" asked Caesar.

"Because it must," said Siggerson impatiently. "Physical laws—"

"What physical laws?" said Caesar. "We've got holes opening in space wherever they want. I think we're damned lucky we didn't fall in."

"Yes," said Kelly with dawning horror. "But who did?"

The three of them stared at one another a moment. Then Caesar slammed his hand down upon a control. The viewscreen wavered into life.

"I see nothing," said 41.

Kelly tensed. "Maybe the other ships got knocked aside just as we did. Put the scanners on a full 360-degree sweep."

Nothing. They were alone as though the *Jefferson* and their sister shuttle had never existed.

Kelly groped backward and dropped into the copilot's seat. He felt drained, hollow, as though all the fight and willpower had been kicked from him. It wasn't supposed to happen like this. His ship was supposed to go through, not the others.

"Dad," he whispered. "Not you. Not you!"

5

Kelly stared at the screen in grim silence for several seconds. Then he said, "Find us a way in, Mr. Siggerson."

"Shouldn't we call—"

"No."

Frowning, Caesar said, "What if we're all wrong about this? What if this is just an area that's like spatial quicksand? Maybe we should—"

"No!" said Kelly.

From the rear of the shuttle Serula said, "Now you know what it's like, Kelly."

He glanced at her, then away. "Look," he said in a more moderate tone to Siggerson. "I'm not interested in conducting a scientific survey here. We know from the admiral's report that ships came through from the other side. They, whoever they are, have deliberately snatched our ships. And apparently they can move their gate. If we had stayed near the *Jefferson*, we would have gone through with her. Now we've got to head back toward her coordinates and hope the gate is still there."

"And if it's moved?" asked Siggerson dourly.

"Then we hunt for it." Kelly sighed. "Listen. We are in a craft that is not designed for deep space travel. We have a limited amount of fuel and a limited amount of air and heat. We cannot get home in this thing. Our only hope of survival is to go after the others."

Silence fell over the shuttle. Finally Caesar stirred.

"Yep," he said. "Looks like we're short on options. Get your rear in gear, Siggie boy. Let's start hunting ourselves some Invaders."

The shuttle limped along. Serula removed her space suit and stored it in silence. No one spoke to her, and she seated herself out of the way. Beaulieu moaned and began to come around. She didn't seem to be hurt other than a bump on the head. 41 rummaged through her kit and sealed up the cut on Kelly's temple. With the blood cleaned off his face and a painkiller damping his headache, Kelly's optimism returned. He figured the Invaders were stealing ships and prisoners in order to learn more about this galaxy before they came through in force. That gave the others a good chance of still being alive.

"41," he said. "Anything else that you can tell us about these Invaders?"

"We don't know they're the same as 41's legend," said Beaulieu, grimacing as she chewed a tablet.

"I think they are the same," said 41.

"How—"

But Kelly held up his hand to silence her. He had learned to respect 41's opinions. The ex-mercenary spoke only when he knew what he was talking about. He never mentioned his past unless absolutely necessary, and Kelly felt sure he wouldn't have brought up the mysterious Old Ones who had raised him if there hadn't been a strong correlation between their legends and the present facts.

"Go ahead, 41," he said. "Is there more you can tell us?"

41's gaze shifted from face to face. He seemed uncomfortable being the center of attention. "I think I have said all that I remember of the tales. The Invaders . . . did not attack alone. Always in threes or multiples of three."

"The tape showed nine ships," said Kelly. "That's useful. Their thinking pattern may be trinary."

"Or they may be trinary beings," said Phila. "Three symbiotic parts forming a whole."

Kelly glanced at 41. "Did the Old Ones ever mention what the Invaders look like?"

"No." 41 thought for a moment, his eyes focused on the past. Finally he gestured a negative. "I can think of nothing else. It was not much spoken of. It was a talking of sad times, when we were to be quiet and respectful within the circle of the temple fire. I was . . . very young. I do not remember much. Except . . ."

"Yes?"

41's eyes lifted slowly to meet Kelly's. "That I feel as though I should do vengeance upon them. It is an . . . old feeling. I do not think it is mine."

Serula leaned forward. "Are you telepathic? Is it a command marker that was placed in your subconscious? You may be triggered by—"

In a blur of movement 41's prong was drawn and all three blades snapped open. Kelly dived forward and clamped a hand on his wrist.

"Take it easy, 41. It's just a question."

41's gaze was locked on Serula with such intensity that for a moment Kelly feared 41 didn't even hear him. Then he eased off, and Kelly released his wrist.

"I don't think you had better talk to him again, Captain," said Kelly. Serula made no reply. He glanced at her sharply and saw that she was pale. She nodded in silence. "41, put away the prong."

41's wrist flexed as he lowered the weapon. His fingers were clamped so tightly upon the haft they trembled. He drew an uneven breath and abruptly sat down.

"I am not a tool," he said roughly. "I am not marked, to

be turned on by unseen hands, for terrible purposes. I am not—"

"I know," said Kelly in sympathy. This wasn't the first time 41 had been accused of such things. It came of being half-Salukan, which seemed to awaken paranoia in some people. "Don't worry about it. Siggerson, how much longer?"

"We're coming up on the position now," replied the pilot. "Scanners are showing nothing peculiar."

"Everyone, get strapped in," said Kelly. "We don't want to be caught unawares again."

They scrambled to comply and sat tensely while Siggerson took them through sweep after sweep.

"Nothing," he muttered. "What now, Kelly? Our fuel reserves are half gone."

"Keep looking," said Kelly.

Siggerson shot him an exasperated look but turned the shuttle into a wider arc. No one spoke. Their faces were tight with suspense. Kelly held down rising impatience. He'd never been much good at waiting. Across from him Phila's small thin fingers kept fidgeting, plucking at the knees of her black and silver uniform, folding the cloth into minuscule pleats, then smoothing it out.

The vibration within the shuttle's structure had grown worse. It was an irregular shake, and each time the shuttle faltered they all grew more conscious of the immensity of space waiting beyond a few centimeters of pyrillium alloy. The temperature within the shuttle had dropped ten degrees. Siggerson was trying to conserve energy. Kelly stared at his hands, keeping his mind blank.

"That's it," said Siggerson, breaking the silence. "We're wasting fuel circling out here. I'm calling Station 4."

"It will take hours for a message to reach them," said Phila. "We don't have that much—"

"Nevertheless," said Siggerson stubbornly. "I'm going to inform them of what's happened."

He waited a moment as though expecting Kelly to stop him, but Kelly did nothing.

"This is Shuttlecraft 2 from the ESS *Jefferson* . . ."

"Anyone care to play poker?" asked Caesar, pulling a deck of cards from his pocket. "The old-fashioned kind?"

"God, Caesar!" said Phila. "How can you think of something as stupid as a game at a time like this?"

"A diversion makes sense," said Beaulieu.

"Yeah," said Caesar, shuffling the cards. "Better than sitting here like a stack of corpses, waiting for the air to run out."

"They don't know we're out here," said Kelly suddenly. "We're too small. Whatever kind of sensor is rigged on the gate, we're not triggering it. Mr. Siggerson, does this shuttle have any kind of armament?"

Caesar hooted. "This crate?"

"No, it does not," said Siggerson. "Your theory makes sense, Kelly, but we have no way to act upon it."

Kelly looked at Caesar. "What have you got? Come on, Samms! You've always got a few gadgets up your sleeve. How about some of that explosive gel?"

"Yo," said Caesar, starting to grin. He opened pockets in his uniform and pulled out three packets of the soft, explosive gel, a cuboid object small enough to be hidden in one palm, a coil of clear filament maybe a millimeter or two thick, and a supply of stylus-shaped detonators.

Caesar looked up. "How big a bang do you want, boss?"

"Big," said Kelly.

Caesar thought for a moment, then he unsnapped his safety harness and began crawling about the deck on his hands and knees. "Where's the engine access hatch?"

Serula pointed to the rear of the shuttle. Caesar went there, followed by Kelly and 41. They helped him spin the big release bolts and lifted the hatch lid. Smoke boiled out, choking them.

Waving it aside, Caesar peered down through the hatchway. "What a piece of junk. I can detach a generator or the heat unit and wire it up with the gel. Short of putting us all in suits and blowing the shuttle herself, which seems to be slightly risky and irresponsible even for you, boss, I don't think I can do better."

Kelly smiled. "Let's get to work."

41 exchanged places with Siggerson at the controls, and the pilot supervised as Kelly and Caesar sweated during the next half hour to extract the heating unit from the engine housing. It was self-contained, possessing a battery pack that could power it for a limited time if the engine failed. Caesar studied it and attached two gel packs to it with precision.

"Why not put them all on it?" asked Siggerson.

"Because, Siggie boy," replied Caesar, slipping the third gel pack back into his pocket, "two is enough to ignite the liquid nitrax in the core of this baby."

"And because Caesar would rather have a bomb than a gun any day," said Kelly.

Caesar smiled at him and patted his creation. "She's ready."

Using an anti-grav prod taken from the repair kit, they maneuvered the heavy heating unit into the airlock. 41 jettisoned it, and a few seconds later the viewscreen showed it tumbling into space.

"Places, everyone," said Kelly. "Siggerson, move us just out of range of the blast, but not too far away."

Caesar gave Siggerson a more precise range. The shuttle shuddered as she came about. Hurriedly they strapped themselves in once more.

Kelly looked at Caesar. "Now."

Caesar activated the detonation. The resulting explosion rocked the shuttle hard. At once Siggerson moved the shuttle in closer.

They waited for ten minutes.

"Nothing," said 41.

Caesar shook his head. "Well, boss. Looks like either we didn't knock hard enough or no one is at home—"

It was like being dropped down a launch chute in a g-force training exercise. One moment they were stationary; the next they were plunging nowhere. Kelly gripped the arms of his seat, thankful for the safety harness that was cutting into him from the tremendous pressure. His flesh felt like it was sliding off his bones. He couldn't breathe. His blood all seemed to be rushing into his skull. Everything blurred around him. Sound distorted into a wall.

He wanted to scream, but he hadn't enough breath. He shut his eyes and felt moisture seeping out around his eyelids. Tears or blood, he couldn't tell. His sinus passages felt as though they were collapsing. Next his skull would cave in. The pressure was going to grind his body to a pulp. He was afraid to force open his eyes, afraid of what he might see, afraid that he couldn't see at all.

Then, as though the shuttle hit the bottom of a deep, black well, they jolted sideways. The horrible pressure eased off. For the first time in interminable seconds Kelly could breathe. He sucked in a lungful of air and cautiously cracked open his eyes.

There was no light. He took his right hand off the armrest and groped with it. For an instant his fingers brushed 41's sleeve, then they passed right through into nothingness.

Kelly gasped. "41?" he said. His voice sounded faint and far away. "41? I think I just put my hand through you. Are you there?"

He heard no reply. Chilled, he snatched back his hand. The shuttle had begun a slow, drifting spin. Kelly swallowed and shut his eyes. His heart was pounding so hard it hurt. Maybe, he thought dizzily as the spin became faster, they had finally gotten themselves into something they couldn't handle.

A distant babble of voices grew louder. At first Kelly strained to hear, until he realized the voices were in his head, an overlay of memories flashing back too fast to comprehend on a fully conscious level.

Another jolt seemed to rattle all his bones together. He

inadvertently bit his tongue and the sharp taste of blood helped him cling to something he could understand.

Blinding light suddenly snapped on, blasting against his shut eyelids. Dazed, Kelly hunched in his seat until he realized that they had stopped moving. Slowly, not certain he wanted to look around, he opened his eyes. His vision was blurred, grainy, not quite in focus until he blinked several times, hard.

He lifted his hands to his face, rubbing it. Around him the shuttle remained intact. The others looked crumpled in their seats. 41 was drenched with sweat, his golden hair matted in damp streaks against his skull. Phila, her eyes squinched tightly shut, was crying with silent sobs that shook her petite frame. Caesar's green eyes stared into space, as vacant as though his mind had ceased to function. Siggerson had slumped over the controls, his shoulder blades making sharp points beneath his uniform. Beaulieu had her head tipped back. She kept saying, "No," over and over. Captain Serula looked unconscious.

Something clanged against the hull, echoing loudly. Kelly jumped and scrambled free of his harness in alarm. The shuttle jerked, nearly knocking him off his feet. He hurried to the controls, grasping Siggerson's shoulder and pulling him upright in his seat to reach them.

Siggerson sighed and opened his eyes. "What did we go through?" he whispered.

"Don't know," replied Kelly, trying to activate the viewscreen. He frowned at their position readings and thumped the console. "Is this working? I know we've moved. That was a hell of a ride somewhere."

"It says we're back where we started." Siggerson frowned and started running checks. "With junker Fleet equipment like this you never know, but everything appears to be in order. This just does not make sense. We can't be at the same coordinates."

"But we are," said Kelly thoughtfully. "Time travel?

Maybe we've been all wrong about this parallel universe theory. Maybe we're dealing with invaders from the past."

"Or the future," said 41.

"Great," said Caesar, rolling his eyes. "I suppose we've fallen into a time loop and are trapped here for the rest of eternity. What do I do now? Rig another bomb? I'm running out of explosive fast, boss."

Kelly ignored his sarcasm. "We definitely went somewhere, even if we're back now. Get these scanners going, will you, Siggerson? I want to know what's happening outside."

The viewscreen wobbled on and displayed a black-hulled ship so vast it filled the screen. Its outlines showed up only because of a faint corona of light around it, and its configuration was an angular wedge, as solid and as featureless as polished obsidian.

Kelly stared, unable to believe what he was seeing. The others crowded around, and Caesar gave a low whistle.

"How big?" whispered Kelly in awe.

"Twenty kilometers across. Four kilometers deep," said Siggerson.

"Yusus," said Caesar, his jaw dropping. "Several space stations would fit in this baby."

"Amazing," said Siggerson. "Even the Minzanese couldn't begin to build a vessel of this size. How do they power her? Do you suppose she can go faster than light? The immense distortion required to push such a huge mass at that velocity would be—"

The clang came again on the hull, and they lurched.

"Commander," said Siggerson in alarm. "Our power drive just cut off."

As if to emphasize his words, the lights went off. Seconds later they came back on, but they were dimmer, running off battery reserve.

Kelly jumped from his chair. "What's happening?"

"We're being towed," said Siggerson.

Kelly stared at the ceiling. "Any way to detach ourselves?"

Siggerson did some checking. "No. I can't locate a tractor beam. Hull sensors register nothing. Nevertheless, we are being pulled away from our position. We are moving toward that alien vessel. It is not natural drift. If we had the *Valiant* instead of this crate we could manage to . . ." His voice trailed off and he didn't complete his sentence.

Kelly glanced around. There was no way he was going to sit here and be towed helplessly into the maw of that behemoth.

"Time for Plan B," he said briskly. "41, break out the weapons. Phila, you distribute the space suits. Caesar, all Fleet shuttles have an emergency access in addition to the main airlock. Find it and loosen it."

Caesar grinned. "Going out the back door? Yes, sir!"

"Care to fill the rest of us in on this Plan B?" asked Beaulieu.

"Standard operating procedure," said Kelly, catching the suit Phila tossed to him and unrolling it with a deft shake. "We are about to confront an unknown species. We provide ourselves with environment, and we put a man on the roof just in case."

"And if their scanners pick up what we're doing?" said Phila. "They're bound to be monitoring us from every angle. What about hull burning?"

"What's that?" asked Beaulieu.

While Phila explained the procedure of scouring a ship's hull of contaminants or foreign bodies before accepting it into a station, Kelly finished pulling on his suit. He checked his nostril plug for fit, allowed a minuscule amount of air to blow from his tanks, checked all levels to make sure the suit had been properly serviced, and tuned the communicator to the one he wore on his wrist.

Meanwhile, Beaulieu was staring at him as though he had lost his mind.

"Hull burning is a risk," said Kelly. "But 41 and I aren't going to be on the hull."

"Oh?" said Beaulieu. Her eyes suddenly widened. "You aren't going to try free floating. Kelly, that's crazy!"

"Yes, it is," he said a bit sharply. "If you will give me a chance to explain, Doctor, I'll do so. We're going to hide inside the power drive units on the tail."

"What!"

A babble broke out as they all tried to speak at once. Coming from the munitions locker, 41 met Kelly's gaze with a slight, unflappable smile. He handed Kelly a plasma pistol with both long- and short-range capability and moved about the shuttle to distribute weapons to the others. Even Caesar came skimming down the rungs bolted to the wall.

"Boss, that's crazy!" he said. "You'd be crisped with radiation in seconds."

"This suit can handle residue levels."

"I'm not talking about residue." Caesar planted himself in front of Kelly. "Those drives—"

"—are shut down," said Kelly. "We'll be fine."

"And if they come back on? We may be under some kind of damping field right now, but you can't count on that."

Kelly glanced at Siggerson. "Shut them down on your board."

Siggerson complied. Kelly activated the charge on his pistol, wishing he had a diehard instead.

"Ready, 41?"

41 was suited, armed, and leaning against the wall by the rungs.

Caesar shook his head. "I got a bad feeling about this stunt, boss. Why not wait until we're in there, then we can all come swarming out together, half from the main airlock and half from the emergency hatch. That way we can—"

"No," said Kelly. "Get your suit on. I want everyone ready for atmosphere loss in sixty seconds. When they pull us in, this is going to be a dead craft."

Serula smiled. "I understand," she said in excitement.

"They'll think that their damping field wiped out everything instead of just the power drives. Clever, Kelly."

"And what about our life signs?" asked Siggerson, hastily stuffing Ouoji inside his suit with him.

"With the suit shields on, we'll be blurred. They won't be able to get a clear reading," said Serula. She eyed Kelly with respect for the first time. "It's a new design in space suits. You've been keeping up on your reading, Commander."

"That's what they pay me for," said Kelly. He noticed that no one had given Serula a gun and frowned. "41, where's the captain's pistol?"

41 straightened from the wall. Fury darkened his face. "She is not to be trusted."

"You will stand down from that remark, operative," snapped Serula.

Caesar stepped between her and 41. "You don't know squat, Fleeter. Nobody stands down in this squad. And you shot him, remember?"

"I did him no harm," said Serula defensively, but her face was red.

"Can it," said Kelly. "We don't have time for arguments. And we need maximum firepower. Give her the gun, 41."

For a moment it seemed that 41 would not obey. But at last with great reluctance he gave her the bi-muzzled pistol. His eyes had turned a flat, dangerous yellow.

Caesar stepped a little closer, violating Serula's personal space. "Just remember whose side you're on. You take any more potshots at any of us, and I'll personally ram this gel pack up your—"

"Caesar," said Kelly sharply.

"Soyo, boss," said Caesar, and moved away from Serula.

Kelly signaled for 41 to start up the ladder. "Siggerson, stand by to jettison the air. Try to move about as little as possible when we go in. Don't start shooting until I give the order."

He shut his face plate and heard the soft hiss as it sealed. His tanked air came on, smelling slightly sour. The others sealed their face plates. 41 waited at the top of the ladder with his hand upon the hatch control. Kelly gave his squad a thumbs-up. Gravely they returned the good luck gesture.

He tapped 41's boot, and 41 opened the hatch. As he and Kelly climbed into the tiny airlock, Kelly heard Caesar muttering over the general comm link: "I'd just as soon stick my arm into a whirl saw as sit in a hot drive tube."

Kelly frowned and started to say something, then bit it back. Caesar had a point, but this plan was the best Kelly could think up at the moment, especially since he hadn't the foggiest idea of what they were up against. In times like this it was better not to think at all. Just get into the best position possible and wait for the right moment to pull the trigger.

Grimly he opened the outer hatch and squeezed out first, leaving 41 to follow. The immense void of space surrounded them, too vast to look at, too incredible to comprehend. Dwarfed by the alien ship ahead of them, Kelly felt totally exposed although he knew he was no more than a mere speck to any watchers inside that enormous craft.

The magnetic plates in his boots locked him to the hull, but he kept a tight handhold at all times as a precaution. Without a tether, boot plates alone just weren't sufficiently reliable, especially with the shuttle moving on a tractor beam.

Carefully he moved to the stern of the shuttle. There, he switched off the magnets in his boots and let his feet float upward. Headfirst, he pulled himself down to the starboard drive tube and crawled inside. There was just enough room for a man his size to fit. He wedged himself securely so that he couldn't float out.

Not daring to use voice on his comm, he tapped a pulse code to 41.

After a short delay that had him sweating, thinking 41

had slipped off and was free floating behind them, 41 pulsed back a reply. He was in position and secure.

Kelly sighed. His throat ached with thirst. His body felt tense and tired and restless for action. The aliens had started it, he reminded himself grimly. With a lot of luck, he and his squad would finish it.

He just wished he knew how.

6

Holborn was working on the third generation of Type 4 cultures when a carrier entered his laboratory. His back was to the door, yet he recognized that stolid footstep pattern and heard the faint hiss of hydraulic levers that lifted and propelled the carrier's legs. The sound never failed to inject a burst of fear into him.

Holborn straightened from his microscope and turned around too quickly, knocking off a petri dish as he did so. The glass shattered upon the floor. Fortunately that particular dish was empty. He had intended it to hold cell smears from the next mutation. Had he broken any of the three other dishes, the whole laboratory would have been contaminated with a deadly viral strain in seconds.

The carrier stopped and bent its head slightly to scan the breakage.

"I'll have it cleaned up in a few minutes," said Holborn. "As soon as I finish with this experiment."

The carrier made no reply, and Holborn wiped his face with an unsteady hand. He knew it was unwise to betray this much nervousness to his masters because they might suspect him of duplicity, but the carriers always made him nervous even when they were empty-handed and serving merely as messengers, as this one was. A simple reason for this little neurosis of his might be that a carrier had trod upon his foot, breaking it, the day he first came to the City.

He had limped ever since, but deep in his heart he knew nothing was that simple. No, his fear was cold and black, growing daily, spreading from deep inside him like a cancer.

The Visci were frightening enough in and of themselves, but they were seldom seen in their true state. And although perhaps a million Visci lived within the City, they were small and shut away in their containers. That left the thousands of robots who maintained the City, manned the ships, operated the time gate, toiled in the laboratories, and served as the arms, legs, eyes, and voice of the Visci.

Holborn was no stranger to sophisticated machinery, certainly, but to have robots as the only visible population left the City an eerie, silent place that wore on his nerves. At first there had been a staff of fourteen coworkers for him to oversee. Most of them had been Therakans and Salukans, captured and brought here under duress. In the past six years all but two of them had died from various causes: overwork, improper nutrition, executions for attempted escape or sabotage. Holborn remained because he was too much a coward to try anything subversive. The fact that he was consumed with trying to solve the problem of the plague both shamed and fascinated him. He hated it here, but he did not really want to leave. He could no longer imagine living anywhere else.

Still, he remained afraid. He might not solve the puzzle quickly enough. He might fail. And his masters did not tolerate failure. Yet if he did not fail, if he found the answer and saved them from the plague that eroded their numbers so mercilessly, what remained for him to do? This had become his life's work. If he saved them, they would go from the City, and might they not leave him here alone with the machines?

Swallowing hard, Holborn faced the glowing lamps that approximated eyes on the carrier and resisted the need to wipe his sweating palms upon his lab smock.

"Yes?" he said sharply. "You are interrupting my work. I have only seconds in which to observe the next mutation—"

"All experiments are being recorded," said the carrier in a toneless, synthesized voice. "Presence requested in observation area."

Experience had taught him it was pointless to argue or try to delay answering a summons. Holborn nodded jerkily. "I will come."

The carrier turned its sleek metal head to scan the overhead lights. "Too bright by twenty watts. Wasteful. I will adjust."

The lights dimmed to a bleary gloom that made the digitalized readouts of the lab equipment glow. Holborn frowned and just managed to hold back a protest. He missed the bright sun of his home world, and he was currently suffering from an irrational aversion to the power-conserving gloom that shrouded most of the City. The robots had their own lamps, so the dim light offered them no difficulties, but each time he left the comforting confines of his laboratory he felt as though he was leaving the only safe area in the City.

Absurd. He must stop assigning living motivations to the robots. This carrier was not luring him out into the avenue in order to murder him. It was escorting him to his summons because he tended to get lost if allowed to wander about the City on his own. Nothing more sinister than that.

Nevertheless, he glanced in appeal at the hunched back of Mevil, toiling over delicate DNA carving.

"Mevil?" he said.

The biotech engineer had not paused when the overhead lights dimmed. He did not look up now. "What?"

"I—" Holborn frowned. What was there to say? Neither Mevil nor Righa liked him. They were not of his species; they had nothing in common with him other than the work itself. "I'll be back soon," he said lamely.

As he passed through the doorway into the avenue of black floor, black walls, black ceiling, all fashioned of metal so strong a cutting diamond could not scratch it and a megaton focused plasma blast could not dent it, a shiver caught him right between his shoulder blades.

The carrier followed him. The lab door locked. Holborn paused, breathing a shade too fast, and the carrier stepped past him to lead the way. Its head casing housed a computer that could process rapidly yet lacked the capacity for independent thought. Its body was ovoid, sleek with a metallic sheen that reflected light. Powerful arms and legs pumped in a stolid, rocking rhythm. They had no casing to disguise the levers and pulleys that operated them.

Holborn followed, listening to the thump and hum of well-lubricated machinery. I will become one, he thought. If I stay here long enough I will mutate just as the cultures are mutating. My processes will be slower, of course, but it will happen. That's where all these robots came from: living tissue ossified into metal.

But even as that last thought occurred to him, he shoved it worriedly away. Delusions, fanciful thoughts, madness.

Shaking hands, a tremor about the heart, burning sensation along his temples, difficulty in focusing on distant objects, irrational phobias: all of that spelled overwork. Possibly it even warned of an imminent collapse. He should stop driving himself so hard. But there was nothing to do here but work or sleep. And his masters wanted a solution so very badly to what was killing them.

It would have taken a day to walk across the City. Instead the carrier came to an intersection of avenues and halted on the scarlet grid square set into the floor. Sighing, trying to master the urge to turn and scuttle into the nearest hiding place, Holborn stepped onto the grid and forced himself to

stand still while the carrier grasped his arms with fingers of
cold black steel. The carrier spoke in binary, and there came
the nauseating sense of displacement that marked teleportation. Holborn shut his eyes quickly.

Seconds later Holborn's arms were released. He opened
his eyes and found himself in the observation area.

The carrier pointed. "Go that way."

Its task accomplished, it shut down until its control
should have other commands for it. Holborn turned away
and started walking in the direction indicated. The observation area was vast, as all areas in the City were. He stayed
near the wall, well away from the windows overlooking the
hanger.

Spaceships of all makes and sizes were berthed here like
exhibits mounted in a case. Their pale hulls gleamed softly
against the darkness. Once he would have gazed out, eager
to see the new additions to the collection. He would have
counted them, wondered about the crews, made mental
notations of their names and registry numbers, compared
the various technologies. That habit had faded from him.

He trudged along, barely glancing out at them, until his
crippled foot ached from the unaccustomed exercise. The
carrier could have teleported him closer, he thought grouchily. Twice he passed immobile carriers, eerie sentinels
frozen in place until they should be needed. Each time he
had to force himself not to break into a run. He kept
imagining that they were watching him, pretending to be
immobile, waiting for him to go past them so that they
could strike at his unprotected back. Sleek, black, faceless
except for their lamps, biped ambulatory, taller than he—
were they humming to life?

Despising himself, he glanced fearfully over his shoulder. They remained shut down. He was safe. He was also
going quietly mad. Should he tell his masters? Ask for
medical assistance, therapy, rest? Or should he go on with
his work? He was close to a breakthrough. If only his mind

didn't burn so much with fatigue, he might come more quickly to the answer.

And if he did find it, his masters would leave him here. He would die alone and purposeless among the machines.

Breaking out in a cold sweat, Holborn paused a moment and rubbed his face. Perhaps the solution had been staring him in the face for several work cycles and he was subconsciously blocking it.

He thought he should return to his laboratory and go over all his notes once again. Coming here was a waste of time. How would he explain to the Visci that he had the answer all this time yet could not see it because of fatigue? They would think he'd withheld it just to let more of them die.

Twisting his hands, he hurried back the way he'd come, forgetting that he'd been summoned. Then a muffled sound caught his attention.

He glanced to his left, and through the window he saw the hangar doors opening. A shuttlecraft was being towed inside. Holborn shook his head. He couldn't be distracted now. He mustn't linger here. He had work to do. He had such a headache. It was this dim light. He couldn't see properly, but when he got back to the laboratory he would have those lights readjusted. And he felt weak suddenly, unable to go on walking, as though all the energy fled his limbs and left him boneless.

Sinking to his knees, he feared he had been gassed for his disobedience. Then he realized it was only hunger. Bending over, he clutched his middle and began to weep, making small mewling sounds that embarrassed him.

Am I crazy, he wondered, kneeling before the vast window while the craft came gliding closer, gleaming a pearly gray against the blackness of space, a nimbus of sheer blue glowing off her outlines from the magnetic field. She was a stubby vessel, too small for deep space going. Earth made, by the look of her.

She came into her berth, looking as though she would penetrate the window and run upon him, crushing him against the bulkhead. But she stopped precisely where she was meant to. Mechanical clamping arms extended to fasten her in place. Her running lights were dead.

Wiping his eyes and face, Holborn wondered if the same could be said about her crew. How much more genetic stock did the Visci need to examine?

He pushed the doubt away. He never questioned the actions or the motives of his masters. It was safest that way.

A nearby teleportation grid shimmered, and nine fighters materialized with their firing arms crossed and their lamps glowing scarlet in the gloom. Metallic giants, they marched along the corridor toward Holborn, who scuttled hastily out of their way.

He knew they would go directly through the airlock and remove the crew from the newly captured shuttlecraft. The crew would then be dispersed to various labs and labeled according to genetic codes. If they offered no different pattern or if their DNA proved resistant to retro-virus 90, they would be terminated. The others would have tissue samples extracted from them and would be kept in a holding pen for as long as samples were needed.

Samples for my work, thought Holborn. He got to his feet and moved reluctantly to the window, drawn almost against his will yet curious to see who had been captured this time. He knew that if he saw their faces he would have nightmares during his next sleep cycle. He always did, and for that reason he usually stayed away from the observation area. The tissue samples and genetic codes were brought to him and he worked with them, finding less torment to his conscience in that anonymity.

The fighters seemed to be inside the shuttle longer than usual. Holborn pressed his face against the icy surface of the glass. He thought he saw movement atop the shuttle and frowned, squinting in an effort to see better. But nothing moved now and he decided he must have been imagining it.

"Holborn."

The voice came out of nowhere and made him jump. He

turned, his pulse hammering in his throat, and saw an ovoid
monitor of black metal hovering perhaps ten centimeters
above his head. Its cam lens descended to eye level to peer
at him. Holborn nibbled on his lips, feeling his mouth dry
out. He remembered now that he was supposed to report to
someone.

"Follow."

The monitor swiveled so that its lens remained fixed upon
him as it turned about and floated away, its anti-grav unit
humming with a gravelly, irregular motor rhythm. Holborn
followed meekly. He didn't mind the eyes so much. That
wasn't consistent of him, for the eyes could watch his
actions much more closely than the carriers whose primary
function was to transport the Visci about, but who said
madness had to be consistent?

The corridor curved about the end of this docking pod
with perhaps sixty or more pods stretching out past it. The
monitor floated up out of the way, and Holborn found himself facing a triad of carriers. Each held a small container
emblazoned with brightly colored crests marking the families and lineages of the Visci within. Holborn recognized
the crest on the center container. No actual name had ever
been given to him, for the Visci had other means of
identification among themselves, but since being touched
by the mind of that particular master, Holborn had always
thought of it as Maon.

Maon had great curiosity and more vigor than most of its
kind. When Holborn first came to the City, Maon sent for
him often to ask questions about humans and their world of
origin. Twice, when Holborn's line of research had failed,
Maon had interceded to save him from termination. Holborn wanted very much to repay Maon by finding an
antidote to the plague.

He swallowed, conscious of being late, of having erred,
of having perhaps offended. Those closed containers had a
sinister air about them, although had one of them opened he
would have gone blank with terror. He had seen Maon only

once, but the memory was forever burned upon his mind. To have it enter him through the nostrils, choking him, smothering him, curling upward through his nasal passages into his brain, pressing the neural centers that controlled him until he was nothing but a puppet, possessed, horrified, dying of asphyxiation and fear, was an experience he never wanted to go through again. It had lasted perhaps seconds, but it seemed an eternity.

"Holborn."

He flinched. The voice was mechanical, belonging to one of the carriers that would speak for its master.

"Observe the shuttlecraft. This is an Earth-made ship?"

Holborn faced the window, where he could observe the shuttle from a new angle. Beside him a squat, dome-shaped robot with ropelike appendages of flexible cable operated a console with elaborate data displays.

"Holborn."

Holborn flinched again, cursing his wandering concentration. "Yes, it is of Earth configuration. Why do the readings not show clear life signs? Is the crew dead?"

"Unknown. The internal scanning tells us they are wearing closed environment containers. What species is like us? What species must exist in sterile conditions? Explain?"

"I can't. I—I mean, they may be in space suits for other reasons. Was the ship damaged during capture? Was its atmosphere lost?"

The communications robot snaked another appendage to a linkup. "Yes, atmosphere was lost. Just as we cannot control proper adhesion of our molecules without environment of certain weight and pressure, humans are also limited to specific atmospheric conditions."

It was not a question. Maon frequently thought aloud. Holborn shifted restlessly, wondering why he had been brought here.

"Unlike all other captured vessels, this one attempted to enter the gate. We do not understand this behavior. Explain it."

Holborn blinked a moment. "Obviously they were searching for the others."

"Others?"

"The captured ships."

"Specifics: equipment recovery?"

"No," said Holborn sharply. "People recovery. Humans value life over machinery."

"Peculiar. The units are armed. Five units are within the craft. Two units are outside. Explain."

Seven men, thought Holborn with an almost hysterical urge to laugh. "It's a rescue mission," he said. "Humans will fight to recover people. They want back all the humans you've captured."

"This is not possible."

"No, but they don't understand that. All they know is that their ships have been disappearing in this sector." Holborn saw movement on top of the shuttle and stepped closer to the window. "They must not be allowed to exchange fire with your fighters. No damage until I've collected my samples."

"Agreed." Maon's carrier stepped closer to the window. "Gas the units inside the shuttle. Leave the two units outside the shuttle unrestrained. We will observe their actions."

Binary commands flashed forth. Holborn continued to watch, forgetting his experiments waiting for him back in the lab. The ones who struggled were the most pathetic. After all, the Visci could not be beaten. The sooner his own species accepted fate, the more of them would survive. They would learn how to serve their new masters. They would adapt. He had.

Yet his palms felt moist, and his heart was beating faster. He touched the ice-cold glass, making little mists of condensation spread out around his fingertips. Fight the machines, he thought. Beat them.

* * *

Right now, however, Kelly lay pressed flat upon the top of the shuttle, his feet hooked to keep him from floating off in the zero gravity of the hangar. His half-baked plan to lead his squad in an assault had fallen apart the moment he saw the phalanx of nine black robots. Each was about three meters tall and a meter wide, possessing powerful batteries and chargers for guts. Their arms ended in muzzles, and they were undoubtedly armored. His squad was tough and game for just about anything, but exchanging fire with warbots was tantamount to quick suicide.

He frowned behind his face plate, trying to find another option.

"Stand by," he tapped on the pulse code.

But the warbots did not immediately enter the shuttle. An ambulatory canister rolled into sight. A metal hose snaked out from its side and hooked onto the air supply feeder.

Alarmed, Kelly nearly shot to his knees. Beside him, 41 clamped a warning hand on his arm. Kelly flattened himself again, feeling sweat trickle along his hairline. They'd be safe enough in the suits.

He tapped information to Caesar. One of the robots worked to break the security code on the airlock. But as the hatch opened, an explosion burst in the midst of the warbots with an intense, eye-searing fireball. Pieces of metal flew in all directions, and the concussion rocked the shuttle slightly.

Kelly and 41 rose to their knees and opened fire on the three remaining warbots that had been toppled but not destroyed by Caesar's little greeting. Kelly's shot scored harmlessly off the central casing of his target. He raised his aim and hit the scarlet lamps in the thing's head. It exploded, and Kelly grinned in satisfaction. He nudged his helmet comm with his chin to activate it, since there was no point in trying to hide now.

"Aim for their eyes, 41."

"No good," said 41 with a grunt. He threw himself flat to dodge a return bolt of energy that shattered the top hull fin.

Metal fragments pelted Kelly, and a sudden drop in internal pressure told him that his suit had been penetrated.

"I'm losing air!"

41 rolled to him, grabbed him by the arm, and threw open the top hatch. Another bolt of energy slagged the hatch into a fused lump. Kelly fired back, taking the head off another bot, only to stare in dismay as it rose to its feet and continued to fire. The only difference was that its aim was more erratic.

"Damn!" said Kelly, ducking again. He scrambled through the hatch headfirst, cursing the tight fit and beginning to cough for air.

The inner hatch was shut. Kelly stamped the control with his heel. It opened beneath him and he dropped into the shuttle with 41 landing on top of him.

The impact stunned him and drove from his lungs what little air remained. He tried to sit up, wheezing frantically. 41 yanked open his face plate, but the only air in the shuttle was the scant trickle coming in from the open airlock. That wasn't enough. Kelly's lungs labored, heaving so hard his nostrils seemed to collapse. Little black spots danced in his vision, blurring the sight of 41 bending over him. His arms flailed as his whole body fought suffocation. But there was no air, no . . .

Something closed over his nose and mouth. Sweet, cold air rushed into his lungs. He clung to the emergency mask, sucking in the air with a frenzy he could not control. 41 gave him a pat and moved away. Kelly heard the scream of shooting still going on around the main hatch. He tried to sit up, but Beaulieu took 41's place beside him, holding him where he was. She handed him a small tank with a hose and nostril clamp. It was gear designed for low-oxygen conditions.

"Put this on," she said over the comm. "I hope it works."

"We blew them to bits, but the damned things won't die!" shouted Caesar over the comm. "Doc, get over here! Phila's—"

Beaulieu scrambled away. Kelly sat up, keeping to the scant cover provided by the seats. Drawing off his helmet, he fitted the nostril clamp into place. For a moment the sensation of suffocating returned, but he fought it off. He didn't have enough air, but he could stay alive on this for a short time.

Grasping his pistol, he crawled around the base of the seats and scrambled to the wall where his squad was taking cover. Two headless bots stood shoulder to shoulder, firing all four arms in blasts of energy that had the hatch rim dripping metal. One side of the hatch was on fire that kept sputtering with fitful pops.

Not enough air for it either, thought Kelly. He felt as though he might pass out.

A hand patted his knee. The person he was crammed against twisted to face him, and he saw Serula's face through the plate of her helmet. "You all right?" she mouthed.

He lifted his thumb. Without his helmet, he had no comm to use. She smiled at him through her face plate, then flung herself past 41 to squeeze off several rounds before retreating.

On Kelly's other side, Beaulieu bent over Phila, who looked small and crumpled upon the floor. Her suit looked intact. Kelly wondered what she'd been hit with.

In any case, they had to do something and fast. They were outgunned all the way around and trapped here like bugs in a bottle.

Do something.

He glanced out quickly and noted that the bots seemed fused in the same firing position. Maybe they had deliberately locked themselves into place, or maybe something had shorted. Any risk was worth sitting here until the air tanks and ammo charges ran dry.

On his stomach Kelly squirmed down the wall, flinching as an energy bolt ricocheted about the interior of the shuttle, striking the seats inches from Beaulieu and knocking charred stuffing everywhere. Kelly went up the rungs and back through the emergency hatch, wheezing for air, his head aching from lack of sufficient oxygen.

Topside, he poked his head out very, very cautiously until he could just glimpse the bots, still firing. The energy bolts filling the shuttle weren't scoring any direct hits, but the interior temperature was climbing. The squad couldn't endure the heat residues forever.

Kelly rested himself for a few seconds despite the urgency gripping him. When his vision cleared, he rested the butt of his pistol upon the scarred hull and aimed with extreme care. The bot closest to him swung its right firing arm in his direction. Kelly squeezed off a shot, and the firing arm shattered right at the joint.

Elation swelled in his throat, but he forced himself to concentrate. When another firing arm swung in his direction, Kelly shattered it as well. That left one armed bot, and following Kelly's lead, someone inside the shuttle began shooting at its firing arms. They got one, and Kelly took care of the other.

Quiet drifted over them. Feeling weary, Kelly dropped down the rung ladder. The squad was dancing around, slapping hands and shoulders. Kelly waved his arms and gestured for them to move.

41 scooped Phila's slight body effortlessly over one shoulder. With Kelly in the lead, they ducked out of the shuttle and hurried warily past the two standing, but disarmed bots, their boots crunching on the shattered pieces of the others.

A blast of Caesar's weapon upon the controls opened the door leading from the hangar. They stepped inside a world of black. Ceilings, walls, floor, all were black metal. Scant illumination was provided.

But there was air. Kelly took great delicious gulps of it, not caring that it smelled faintly of molded apples, ozone, and lubricant. He glanced over his shoulder at Beaulieu.

She opened her face plate, and he said, "Is this air safe, or does it have gas?"

"Safe," she said.

He unhooked his nostril clamp, and the others opened their face plates.

"Well, we're in," said Kelly, not sure that was a good thing. "We can't just stand here and wait for the next batch of reinforcements. We need to clear this corridor, then we've got to locate the crews of those—"

"Whoa, boss," said Caesar, pointing down the corridor. "Here comes trouble."

They turned, and Kelly saw another phalanx of warbots coming. Metal feet rang upon metal floor in perfect cadence. His heart sank. Last time was mostly luck. This time they were bunched up in this corridor with nowhere to go and not nine warbots coming at them, but twelve.

"Surrender," said a synthesized voice. "Put down all weapons."

"Then what?" muttered Caesar. "They blow us away without any resistance? To hell with this."

Kelly looked at the squad's faces and saw the same thing: anger, resentment, and a gritty determination to resist. He looked at the approaching warbots and saw their firing arms locking into position.

"Right," he said. "To hell with it."

And he opened fire.

7

It wasn't suicide. Just as the squad opened fire, a forcefield shimmered across the corridor between them and the approaching warbots. It didn't reflect the squad's shots; instead it absorbed them.

"Cease fire!" said Kelly.

They obeyed, and stood there tensely to see what the warbots would do. Probably the forcefield would drop to allow the warbots to slaughter them.

"Move," said Kelly, gesturing behind him. "Down the corridor."

"Boss, it ain't going to do no good—"

"Do it."

Cautiously Caesar stepped back, as did 41, still hampered by carrying Phila. Beaulieu and Serula moved closer to the walls. Siggerson hovered near Kelly.

The warbots halted on the other side of the forcefield. Kelly frowned as he took a step back, then another. This was as weird as hell. He had the certain feeling that he was being watched, perhaps even toyed with.

Kelly glanced around and up at the ceiling. Beams of light came on there, dazzling him. They played over him and the others.

"My pistol!" said Siggerson, throwing his upon the floor.

About then Kelly's grew so hot to the touch he could no longer hold it. He tried to master instinct, telling himself that it was just a mind trick, but failed. His weapon went clattering to the floor as well. His palm stung, and the skin turned red and looked slightly blistered. No mind trick, after all. The pistol had really been hot.

The forcefield dropped. The warbots stepped forward. Kelly felt a jerk of fear. He turned to give fresh orders to his squad and saw a forcefield shimmering behind them.

"We're trapped!" said Caesar.

"Maybe we'd better surrender," said Siggerson.

"It won't help," said Kelly. "Either way they mean to kill us."

In perfect step the warbots drew close enough for Kelly to hear the low whirs as their firing arms flared muzzles, revealing long, wickedly barbed darts perhaps the length of Kelly's hand, fitted on spring launchers. His mouth dried out, and his heart began to wham hard against his ribs. There was something primitive and cruel about those darts. He imagined one of them embedded in his chest, filling him with agony while he died slowly and horribly of blood loss. He'd rather be slagged.

A wave of malevolence from something washed over him. For a moment he thought only of the hopelessness of their situation. It would be better to stand quietly and accept their fate.

A hoarse cry from 41 behind him snapped Kelly from his momentary trance. He glanced at Siggerson and saw him staring glassy-eyed at nothing. The others were likewise frozen, except for 41 who shrugged Phila to the ground and came running forward like a wild thing. At the same time the warbots halted less than two meters away. Kelly heard a hissing sound and hastily held his breath.

He grabbed Siggerson and shook him hard, but the pilot didn't snap out of it. Beaulieu didn't respond either. Kelly gave up on the others. 41 passed him and ran between two of the warbots, dodging his way through the others that could not turn to get a clear shot at him in those close quarters. Kelly started after him in the same way, pushing himself to move faster and faster, praying his feet wouldn't tangle as he dodged and twisted and ducked his way through the gigantic robots. One firing arm swung down across his shoulders, driving him to his knees.

Gasping and stunned, Kelly tried to pull himself up and get going but his legs were rubber. His mind and body seemed totally disconnected. He fought not to pass out.

By the time his mind cleared, it was too late for him. A cable had been wound around his ankles, and he was tied to a warbot. It turned slowly, dragging him on the floor.

Ahead, 41 had almost cleared the last row of warbots. He ran with an agility remarkable in someone of his height, his blond hair streaming from his shoulders.

Kelly sat up, straining to see through the forest of metal legs. "Go for it! You can do it, 41!" he yelled.

But the gas was everywhere, hissing louder from invisible vents as it filled the corridor with a milky fog. Kelly saw 41 make it beyond the warbots, then abruptly stumble. A warbot shot a cable from its side, and the cable snaked deftly about 41's legs, yanking him off his feet. 41 yelled something in his own language, which never translated no matter how often the lab boys tinkered with the Hawk translator implants. He fought like a wild thing, twisting about and using his prong to hack at the cable. But before he could cut himself free, the warbot that had captured him struck him with its firing arm. 41 crumpled and lay still.

"No!" said Kelly.

He flailed about, but the gas sapped his strength. It smelled of apples, with a sour bite of something unpleasant underneath. Kelly coughed, foggily wondering how aliens from another dimension could know about apples. He sank down, winded and weak. His head thudded upon the polished black floor, but he scarcely felt the impact.

A voice blared over a speaker, and the warbots parted in half to move against the wall in rows facing each other. Kelly was aware of this on only the dimmest level. He wanted to stay awake, wanted to see the chief bug coming to gloat over them. But his eyes were leaden and his head roared as though it had been submerged in water. He slid deep into darkness.

He awakened with a start, dreaming that something had him by the throat. He wanted desperately to be sick. He found himself strapped on his back on a steel table that felt icy cold through his tunic. A restraint strap circled his throat and more straps held his wrists and ankles. He swallowed hard, forcing down his gorge, and waited for the clammy sweats to leave him.

The throat restraint was loose enough to permit him to turn his head. In one direction he saw what was obviously a laboratory. It was fitted with microscopes, lasers, biocomputers, data sorters, miniature cryogenic chambers, and other pieces of equipment that Kelly could not identify. In the other direction he saw an unconscious 41 lying strapped upon a steel table as he was.

Kelly lifted his head as far as the strap would allow. "41," he said softly but urgently. "41, wake up."

"Do not disturb him," said an unfamiliar voice. "He is in light trance, and it has taken half a work cycle to get the chemical balance exactly right."

A human male in a lab smock came into Kelly's line of vision. He was a short man, very thin and stooped. His dark hair hung in untidy streaks across his wide brow. His skin had the pallid, doughy texture that came from no exercise, improper food, and a lack of sunshine. His eyes looked tired, bloodshot. He blinked rapidly and often.

Kelly stared at him in astonishment. "Who are you? What are you doing here? Are you off one of the ships in

Blue Squadron? If so, how did you manage to become more than a prisoner? What are you doing out of uniform?"

"I am Dr. Holborn, and I do not belong in uniform," said the stranger irritably. "I have no connection to your stupid military organizations. I am here by choice."

He picked up a syringe and plugged a module of murky green liquid into it.

Kelly watched him with a frown, not liking any of this. "Just exactly what is this place? We were engaged in routine rescue work when we were—"

"Save your story for Maon," said Holborn. "It will be here soon enough. I have no time for conversation. This whole matter is taking me from my work. I have lost data on an entire generation, and today's experiments will have to be started over from scratch."

He administered the full dosage to 41, who twitched as though in pain. Kelly jerked angrily against his restraints. "What are you doing to him?"

"Getting him ready for interrogation. Be quiet, or Maon may decide to talk to you directly as well." Holborn paused and looked at Kelly. "I assure you it is not pleasant. Be thankful that at this moment it shows no interest in you."

"Where's the rest of my squad? What have you done to them?"

Holborn glanced up from 41. "I have done nothing to them. I daresay they have been taken to the holding area. That's routine for all—"

He broke off with a frown, but Kelly tugged impatiently at his restraints.

"Routine, is it?" he said grimly. "Meaning that the crew of Blue Squadron is here somewhere? Meaning that the *Jefferson*'s crew is here too? What's the purpose of this piracy? What—"

Holborn looked past Kelly, and the change in his expression to one of fearful subservience made Kelly break off. Kelly looked in that direction and saw a robot entering the lab. It carried a box approximately seventeen centimeters square.

"Are preparations finished?" asked the robot, coming to a halt near 41.

Holborn stepped back. "Yes, Maon."

"We are displeased to see this unit appear among us," said the robot. "We thought all Svetzin had been terminated in the time of our current investigations."

"Hey!" said Kelly in alarm. "He's not Svetzin. He's half human and half Salukan."

The robot's head swiveled in Kelly's direction. "What is this unit that speaks outside the order?"

"I'm Commander Bryan Kelly of the Allied Intelligence Special Operations branch. That is 41, one of my operatives. We're here investigating the disappearance of six Alliance starships. Piracy is a serious crime—"

"The Kelly unit is human such as yourself, Holborn."

"Yes," said Holborn.

"Rebellious. It accuses us of crimes. The genetic collections?"

"Yes. I told you these men would be interested in recovering people."

Maon remained silent for a few moments. "Military."

"Yes, Maon," said Holborn.

"Kelly," said Maon's synthetic voice. "Trickery and lies. We have observed another unit called Kelly."

"My father," Kelly said eagerly. "Admiral—"

"Holborn," broke in Maon. "Explain father."

Holborn did so in succinct scientific terms. And what about love? thought Kelly. Love and pride and trying to emulate the old man until you were old enough to know you could never fill his shoes?

"Same genetic pattern," said Maon. "This unit is therefore a duplicate and unnecessary."

"Perhaps," said Holborn before Kelly could react. "It depends on the parental cross. I still want a tissue sample."

The robot did not reply. Instead it moved closer to 41. A

series of muted flashes passed across its twin lamps. Then it bent slightly and set the box upon 41's torso.

"Too long," said Maon. "Too long since we have ridden a Svetzin. This one has come to us from the past, seeking to find our hiding place, but we shall turn its guile upon it and use its mind to discover the pathway back to its origin. And we shall destroy the Svetzin again."

"No," said Kelly in frustration, fighting his restraints although he knew it was futile. "You've got it wrong. He's not a—"

The lid of the box raised by itself as though opened from within. Something black and amorphous slopped over the side, flowing down onto 41's chest. It looked like greasy liquid, yet it *moved*, slowly and with purpose. The part that ran down 41's side to the table drew back up to the top of 41's chest. It left no stain behind it. Watching it, Kelly was struck by the sense of intent emanating from it.

"Holborn!" he said sharply. "What is that?"

Holborn was watching with a mixture of distaste and fascination. His eyes moved briefly to Kelly. "Maon."

Kelly blinked, swiftly readjusting his assumptions. The robot then was just a means of transportation. But what kind of being was this thing? And what was it going to do to 41?

Maon was spreading toward 41's chin. It spilled along his throat, pulled itself together, and moved onto 41's face. 41 twitched as part of Maon flowed into his mouth.

"No!" cried Kelly. "Holborn, you must stop it! In God's name, man, it will smother him!"

"No, it won't," said Holborn softly, holding his own mouth open. His lips worked as more of Maon flowed into 41.

Sickened, Kelly watched helplessly as the black liquid covered 41's face, filling his mouth and nostrils, coating his eyes. 41 jerked against the restraints, and Kelly cried out again.

"Stop it! Why won't you stop it? What kind of monster are you to let a man die this way?"

Maon vanished into 41, leaving no trace of its passage. Sweat broke out upon 41's face. His body convulsed violently, and Kelly could feel 41's pain grinding beneath his own breast.

"No!" he called, aware of the futility of his own voice but unable to remain silent. "41! 41!"

Adrenaline gave Kelly enough strength to snap the restraint on his right wrist. Hope surged through him. If he could just get free, somehow he'd find a way to get that thing out of 41 before it was too late.

Get free. Dammit, get free.

He clawed at the strap circling his throat. Holborn noticed and rushed toward him in alarm. But Kelly couldn't get the strap loosened. His fingers slid uselessly over the smooth material, finding no weakness, finding no fastening within reach. He coughed, but only the sudden realization that his air was being cut off made him ease off the pressure. Choking, that was what 41 was doing. The straps cut into 41's wrists and throat as he thrashed. He made a horrible noise somewhere between a retch and a sob. Abruptly his back crashed against the table and he lay still.

Kelly stared at him, unable to believe it, not wanting to believe, thinking that if he just went on refusing to believe it wouldn't be true.

A sweaty sheen gilded 41's face, a sheen now drying to leave his features drawn and smaller.

Kelly opened his mouth, but could utter nothing. His free hand curled into a fist and he felt choked as though he had swallowed something webby that stuck to the walls of his throat.

Holborn bent over 41 briefly, checking for the vital signs that were not there. The impersonal touch of his hands upon 41, the very inertness of 41's body, brought an objectivity to Kelly that he did not want. He didn't want to see 41 as a body, dammit. Not an object to be handled ceremoniously and disposed of.

"Maon has gone straight to the brain this time," said

Holborn. His voice seemed too brittle for the air. "Amazing how the Visci are able to flatten themselves to thicknesses of mere millimeters. Of course the cavities behind the eyes allow the quickest access inside the cranium to the back of the skull. Sometimes they want to explore other areas such as the torso cavity although access through exploding the lungs is always fatal to the host subject. Maon isn't exploring today, however. He was probably able to touch all the brain centers, rather like an additional membrane. The Visci are fascinating beings, aren't they?"

41 lay as still as sun-colored stone.

"No," Kelly whispered. "My friend."

Holborn came and bent over Kelly, snagging his wrist back under the restraint. "I am going to move you into the adjoining room for sample extractions. Don't worry. It won't be painful."

Kelly wanted to spit in his face. "Damn you! That—that *blob* just murdered him and you did nothing to stop it."

Holborn stared at him without comprehension. "You do not understand. The Visci cannot be stopped. They are greater than us. More evolved. They—"

"I don't care if their IQ measures one thousand! They still kill, and that makes them no better than you or me."

Holborn glanced fearfully around as though expecting them to be overheard. "You must be quiet or you will be terminated."

"Killed," said Kelly through his teeth. "Just say killed, dammit. Not terminated. Not turned off. I'm not a machine. I'm a man."

"Y-yes, I—I know," said Holborn, glancing back at the immobile robot that had carried Maon into the room. It appeared deactivated, but at the moment Kelly didn't care one way or the other. He wanted to rip off his bonds and take this place apart. And he would, given half a chance.

Holborn switched on the anti-grav and propelled Kelly's gurney into the next room, which was larger than the first.

The door closed behind him. Kelly closed his eyes, shutting off the memories of 41.

Holborn paused and leaned close to Kelly. "I'm sorry," he said very, very softly. His weak eyes filled with compassion. "Sorry for you and your friend. It's . . . they're dying, you see. We must find a cure soon. Please don't judge them until you understand."

"How can I understand?" said Kelly in a voice like iron. "How does killing my friend help them live? Why are they taking our ships? Why do they need our ships when they have technology such as this?"

"It isn't the ships they want; it's the people. Genetic stock for my studies."

Holborn moved to a viewscreen and activated it, then turned Kelly's table where he could see the graphs displayed. "They have a method—I don't understand it—of dimensional travel."

"Time travel," said Kelly.

"If you like although that's not very precise. This graph, here and here, do you see how the indexes vary? They punch through to different times and take samples."

"Why? We're totally different species," said Kelly. "How could any of this help them?"

"It will," said Holborn fervently. "I'm very close to a breakthrough. With the plague stopped, they can begin expansion again, rebuild their empire, achieve—"

"Never mind the political rhetoric. Where do they come from?"

"I do not know."

"Are they the same invading force defeated by the Svetzin? Maon called 41 a Svetzin, but he isn't—wasn't."

Holborn glanced nervously at the ceiling. "Your friend had received mental training from the Svetzin. For Maon, that is enough to make him one."

"But that's impossible!" said Kelly. "The Svetzin have been extinct for a thousand years."

"Yes, the Visci chose your time for that reason. Svetzin

are long-lived creatures, but even they cannot linger forever. Humankind, even the Salukans, are not as strong. When Earth is cleansed—"

Holborn blinked rapidly and broke off. Kelly stared at him, feeling alarm, desperate to know more.

"Go on," he said. "What about Earth? What do you mean, cleansed?"

"I cannot tell you."

"You must! Dammit, Holborn, you're human too."

"I am a scientist," said Holborn. "I have my work."

"That's bull and you know it." Kelly paused a moment, seeing the evasion in Holborn's eyes. On a hunch he said, "When do you come from?"

"I—I don't remember."

"Yes, you do! Tell me, Holborn."

"I c-can't."

"Tell me."

Holborn looked at Kelly, then began to cry. "When I first came here, Maon entered my mind. He t-took that knowledge from me. He t-took everything from me except how to do my work. Don't you see? My God, don't you see how alone I am here? Just these damned machines everywhere. *Everywhere*. I haven't even my memories for companionship."

Holborn buried his face in his hands. The sound of his crying was ugly, pathetic. Kelly frowned at him, realizing he was no enemy, not this feeble, emaciated man who was just as much a prisoner as the rest of them, perhaps more so.

"How long have you been here?" asked Kelly quietly.

"Years," said Holborn, his voice muffled against his hands. "I've lost count. There's so much work to do. Most of my helpers died. I can't—"

"Holborn, get hold of yourself. We'll help you," said Kelly. "Help us get out of here and we'll take you with us."

Holborn shook his head fearfully. "No. Shut up. Don't say such things. If they're listening they might believe I would consider your offer."

"Of course you'll consider it. You belong with us, Holborn. Not with these blobs and their robots. You know that."

"No!" Holborn backed away from Kelly. "I serve my masters. I believe in their right to exist, to survive. I won't help you."

"What are they going to do to Earth, Holborn?"

"Clean it of other life forms. Live there until their world is safe of the plague."

Kelly felt cold along his spine. His hatred of the Visci turned blacker. "You mean exterminate the population."

"No, no, they won't do that. They aren't barbarians, Kelly. You don't understand them. There are other worlds for humans to live on. Other places—"

"Earth is *ours*."

"It has oceans, you see. Wonderful, life-giving oceans. The pH balance can be altered to suit the Visci. They need it. Just for a while. Just until they are healthy again."

"Altering Earth's oceans will kill the planet. You know that. Then they'll go out and conquer the rest of the galaxy," said Kelly coldly. "No way. Wise up, Holborn. You're living in a dream world."

Holborn glanced nervously at the ceiling and straightened away from Kelly. "You are wrong, Kelly. You're upset and you are saying things that are not true. You are twisting everything, trying to confuse me. I won't help you. I won't listen to you."

"Holborn, I'm a man. Just like you. Are you going to trust the Visci more than a fellow human? *Are you?*"

Holborn was shaking visibly. Kelly felt sorry for him, but not enough to stop.

"When our time as guinea pigs is over, what are they going to do with us? Send us back? Or dispose of us? I know what I think, Holborn. You're going to be alone again, one lone man among all these machines. Think about it, Holborn. Decide whose side you're on."

Holborn's face reddened. "Not yours," he said angrily. "I've seen your future, Kelly! You have none!"

"Holborn—"

But the scientist hurried away to gather his equipment for the samples and did not speak again despite all of Kelly's efforts to provoke and persuade him.

At last Kelly left him alone and lay there in silence. The blood and tissue extractions were painful. Holborn made no attempt to be gentle. But Kelly had other things to think about than physical discomfort. He'd learned enough to know it was urgent that they stop the Visci here and now. Getting away had to come second.

First he had to somehow rejoin his squad, if any of the rest of them were still alive. Then they were going to rip this place apart, taking their revenge on the Visci however they found it.

Kelly put his grief and anger to work for him as he created a plan. The Visci had been beaten once. They could be beaten again. Those blobs were going to regret the day they decided to meddle with humans.

8

Pain, the clawing madness of it. The suffocating nearness of an other. *Thoughts meshing unwillingly. Flashes of mathematical symbols, blurry images, concepts in colors too brilliant to bear. And the pain, always the pain. Entwining through him in a radius from his mind. Sickly tendrils of control. No way to fight. No way of escape.*

One master.
One subject.
Two struggling.
The pain . . . horrible, blinding, intensifying.
Loss.
Surrender.
One.

9

Caesar and Phila sat on a metal floor that was bone-numbing cold and harder than a Vynerian angel's pelvis. They had forcefields for walls, active, not passive, force-fields that crackled viciously if you got within centimeters of them and just about crisped your fingers off if you touched them. Caesar much preferred the passive kind that simply stood there, bending a bit beneath your weight if you leaned on them while their low vibrational energy waves gave you a massage.

"How long have we been here?" demanded Phila, getting up to start pacing again. She had a nasty bruise on her temple. "My chron has stopped."

"So's mine," said Caesar. "Look, toots. If you want to count seconds, go ahead. What we ought to be thinking about is how to get out of this cage."

"I *am*." Phila swept past him, striding hard. The walls crackled ominously as she passed them. "Look there and there. See them?"

"See what?"

"No! Look at the floor. Did that gas dissolve your brain cells?"

Caesar looked at the floor in each of the four corners. "Yo," he said. "I see the beam sets."

"Right." She squatted in the center of their cage and faced him at eye level. "Beam sets. The circuit running this field has to interconnect to form walls. Otherwise it would just keep running in a straight line. Each connection point marks a corner. So if we disrupt that—"

"Tell me how, kid, and I'll kiss your feet."

Phila grinned and pulled out her prong. "The bots didn't take this. No circuits so it didn't register on their sensors. You can be too sophisticated, now, can't you?"

"Yeah." It was Caesar's turn to be impatient. "So they're dumb about a few things. But if you start prying on a beam set with a knife blade, you're going to be one crispy cookie."

Phila snorted and got down on her stomach. She scooted across the floor until her nose was almost to one of the beam sets. It was fist-sized, very slightly raised above the level of the floor with a thin crack running around it that showed it could descend to floor level when deactivated. Phila released only one blade of her prong and inserted the sharp tip into the crack with surgical precision.

The hair prickled on the back of Caesar's neck. He moved prudently to the opposite corner to watch. Phila's head went up. She laid down her prong.

"Caesar, you idiot! Not the opposite corner. If I slip and set off sparks, they will always go in a diagonal. Don't you know anything?"

Caesar blinked and hastily scrambled to a new position. "You're Miss Dynamo. I just blow things up. Is this spot okay?"

"Yeah. You could start on one yourself. Just pry it out with one sharp snap. Get enough leverage and—"

"Never mind. You do it. I don't need my brain juiced, thanks."

She grinned at him, taking no offense at his refusal to help. With her tongue between her teeth, she resumed work. Caesar figured if she got electrocuted she'd bite off her tongue. The notion made him faintly queasy. He looked away, wishing she'd hurry, hoping she didn't kill herself, wondering how long it would take.

A loud spitting of sparks made him jump. He looked around in time to see blue energy, live and terrifying, arc across the cage, missing Phila by such a narrow margin it made the hair on her head stand up from its charge. Now he understood why she'd lain so flat. She scrambled right to the next corner, leaving Caesar no choice but to move right also. Which put him in the corner she'd just jimmied, where all the short sparks were crackling and fizzing. He felt like his fingernails were going to curl off in the backlash.

"Hurry up!" he shouted.

A blinding flash answered him. For a moment he could see nothing but stark whiteness that seared his eyeballs and left him clutching his face. The crackling stopped although his ears were buzzing so much he barely registered the drop in energy. Purple bars seemed branded on the inside of his eyelids.

"We're out of our cage," said Phila smugly.

Caesar rose to his feet, still pressing his hands to his eyes. "Great. I'm also blinded for life. Somehow the cage was better."

"What did you do, stare right at the beam set when I pried it out? *Mandale*, that was pretty stupid."

"Yeah, tell me about it." His eyes were streaming tears, wetting his palms.

She took his arm in a grip surprisingly strong for her small hands and maneuvered him a short distance. "Now. If they recircuit and raise the field again, we won't be inside. I've seen too many idiots stand by and be caught again just because they forgot to leave their cage. Oh, Caesar, for God's sake. Stop being such a baby."

She pulled down his hands and he stood with his eyes squeezed tightly shut, tears still streaming.

"Open them."

"Not yet."

"*Open* them."

He turned his face to her. "Not *yet*, dammit! I've experienced enough explosion blindness to know you don't rush. If my optic nerves are just stunned, they need to be left alone for a few minutes. The quicker I try to use them, the longer it will take. If they're really damaged—"

Phila's hand tightened on his arm. "Something's coming. This way."

Caesar turned clumsily, trying not to fight his blindness, trying to let her guide him. He wanted to grope. He felt terribly cautious. He had the sensation that he might fall at any moment, that there were obstacles in his path to stumble over. But he kept telling himself to trust Phila, to just run beside her, *trust* her.

"Here," she whispered, jerking him to a halt so suddenly he nearly overbalanced. She tugged him left, caught his other arm so that he sensed her standing close in front of him. He caught a whiff of her hair, smelling as though it had been lightly singed.

She backed away from him, pulling him after her. He detected a difference in air temperature. Slightly warmer. The air smelled stale. His shoulder brushed a wall. He flinched.

"What—"

"Hush!" she whispered. "Quiet. We're in a bulkhead cavity. Don't speak."

He waited, straining to listen. In the distance came cadenced footsteps. Robot. His mouth went dry. They were in for it now.

But it went on by as though their escape did not matter.

When the sound of it faded, Phila let out her breath and sagged against him. Ordinarily he enjoyed females clinging to his chest. But Phila was like a kid sister, and about as appealing. He gave her a brief hug, then pushed free.

The whiteness behind his eyelids was fading, becoming dark, becoming normal. Relief washed over him. His luck of the Irish still held.

"I don't understand," Phila was saying. "It walked right through the area where our cage was and never seemed to notice."

"Was it a rolling cannon, or something else?" Caesar rubbed his eyes, smiled, and opened them. He saw total blackness.

"Something else," Phila said. "Just a bipedal robot, unarmed and not as big as the others. It was carrying a small box. I guess it wasn't programmed to observe anything in this area. But you'd think we'd be under surveillance. You'd think by now the sensors would have registered a forcefield failure. This is weird."

Caesar didn't answer. He kept blinking into the darkness, straining to see even the faintest glimmer of light. His pupils must be dilated to the rims, but nothing came in. The luck of the Irish sagged from him. He felt old, quiet, and without confidence.

"Phila," he said, knowing that if he told her, if he said it aloud that would make it true. "I'm really—"

"Come on," she said, brushing past him. "Let's get out of this bolt hole and see if we can find the others."

She caught his hand and tugged him after her. He turned and followed, bumping into the bulkhead. Phila fumbled about and stopped in front of him.

"Damn!" she said. "All the lights have gone out. I can't see anything."

"Nothing?"

"Not one single thing. The darkness is total. Do you think they'll shut off the air and heat as well?"

Caesar didn't answer. He brought his palm up to the tip of his nose and spread his fingers wide. Could he see it? No, but maybe his eyes were okay. He couldn't test them now, so in the meantime he was going to believe they were fine. It was the only way to loosen that painful knot inside his chest.

"Orient yourself," he told Phila. "Put your back to the wall. Which way did we come from?"

"Starboard," she said.

"Take my hand."

They clasped hands tightly, equal now.

"Go port," said Caesar. "Always keep your hand on the wall."

"What if we come to a dead end?" Her voice was small and not as impatient as usual.

"Naw," said Caesar with forced cheerfulness. "We're following that bot, remember? Do you think bots just cruise this place for the fun of it? What would they be doing that for? Trying to pick up shebots?"

"Caesar, that is a very bad joke."

Her voice sounded less scared. Caesar grinned to himself in the darkness, wishing someone would tell him bad jokes to cheer him up. He could sure use a big shot of reassurance right now. Because he didn't like this one bit, this groping along like two helpless grunts.

"I think we ought to have our prongs ready," said Phila.

"For what? You going to unscrew an arm or two? Remember, toots. We haven't seen one living being in this place since we got here."

"I know. It's spooky. Do you figure this whole ship is automated?"

"Who knows? It's so big we may never get to where the people are. Maybe we're down in the hold or something. Maybe this is just the brig. Maybe in about ten kilometers we'll come to a duty station."

She mumbled something rude, but it was too low for Caesar to catch.

After that they walked in silence for what seemed like forever.

"Caesar," said Phila, making him jump. "There's no more wall."

"What? What are you talking about? There has to be a wall."

"I've lost it. *Caesar*—"

He gripped the fabric of her sleeve. "Calm down. Just calm down."

"I am calm," she said in a lower voice. "Sorry. It's a sharp corner. Watch it!"

She jerked backward into him, nearly knocking him off his feet. He clutched her with both hands.

"What the hell are you doing?"

He could hear her breathing in short, jerky catches.

"I . . . touched something."

"Something like what? Come on, Mohatsa. Pull yourself together. You're supposed to be the original firecracker, not some quaking, helpless—"

"All right!" she said in fury, elbowing him in the stomach. "I don't like the dark, okay? I got buried alive as a kid when we were hiding in the trenches during a Jostic raid. It bothers me a little, okay? I think I'm doing pretty good not to be screaming right now."

"Yusus." Caesar blew out a breath. "I'm sorry. Sorry. Okay? Just calm down. What did you touch?"

"Something oozy, like liquid only thicker than that, about like warm pudding."

"On the wall?"

"Look, Samms, I am not making this up."

"Right. Sure. There's some warm pudding on the wall of an alien spacecraft the size of a city." But Caesar's whole attention wasn't on his sarcasm. As he spoke he stepped past her to get in front, still keeping one hand firmly on her sleeve while he groped with the other. He found the corner and slid his fingers around it.

For an instant he felt nothing but solid metal wall. Then his hand plunged into something warm and soft and oozy, something that pulsed against his fingers. And a feeling of hatred washed over him in a wave powerful enough to make him break out in a cold sweat. He snatched back his hand and as it left the thing it made a dull sucking noise.

Caesar staggered back, nearly mashing Phila into the wall. He let go of her and held his hand, gripping it hard as though to be sure it was still there. Surprisingly it wasn't wet. But the thing's warmth still tingled on his flesh. He flexed his hand uneasily.

"Merciful Mary," he whispered, for once swearing sincerely. "What the devil is it?"

"I don't know," said Phila nervously. "And I don't want to find out. Did you feel something from it? Did you get the idea that it doesn't want us here?"

"Yeah," said Caesar. "I think we just met our first life form. The robots were nicer."

"What do we do? It hasn't sounded an alarm."

"Not one we can sense anyway," said Caesar dourly. "Somehow, I don't think it talks or hears or has alarm sirens."

"Will you stop babbling? It knows we're here. We can't just stand around flat-footed and wait for those bots to come pick us up."

She had a point. Caesar fumbled down her arm and found her hand. Grasping it tightly, he said, "Put your other hand on the wall and I'll try to cross the intersection of these corridors."

He started edging his way out there into the middle, his free hand held out slightly ahead of him in case he bumped into anything. Phila yanked him back.

"Caesar, you're going the wrong way. You're headed back the way we just came."

"You sure?"

"Yes! Don't argue. You'll get me confused. Here, you stand by the wall and let me try it."

"I don't think you're—"

"Yes, I am. Now shut up and let me do it."

He gave in, feeling more than a little foolish and wondering how long it would be until the bots got here with bazookas sprouting from their navels and axes for hands. He shivered and felt his forehead. He was stressing out; he had better get himself together.

"I need some more slack," said Phila.

"Slack? It's my arm you're talking about. I can't pay it out like a rope."

"Well, move farther from the wall then. Just don't lose it."

Grumbling, he shifted his position slightly, just keeping his fingertips on the wall. He couldn't help but wonder if little oozy might decide to come on around the corner. He shuddered.

Just then there came a muted flash of light that might as well have been blinding for what it did to his dilated pupils. He cried out, dropping Phila's hand to cover his eyes in a purely reflexive move. In that instant of sight, however, he had seen her standing on a grid painted crimson with a nimbus of light flashing out all around her. Her long black hair stood on end in a broad fan behind her skull, and on her small face was a look of utter terror.

She screamed, then the lights went out again and Caesar was once more plunged into darkness.

"God, what was that! Phila? Phila? Hey!"

She didn't answer. Swearing, he pushed himself in the direction he'd last seen her, but his outstretched hands found nothing. She was gone as though she'd been swallowed up.

Caesar stood there, turning about and turning about. "Phila? What did you do, fall into a teleport field?"

Nothing answered him. But the lights flashed on again, making him cringe even as a part of him rejoiced at having his sight back. He had an instant to look down and see that he was standing on the grid.

He knew then what it was and what had happened to Phila. The question was, where had she teleported to? Another part of the ship, or into space?

Dumb thing to think of now, he told himself. And he vanished.

10

Beaulieu knew a DNA coding chamber when she saw one. She stood in a line of Alliance Fleet personnel, most of whom were suffering hunger, cold, and the side effects of experimentation. They had all been stunned lightly, just enough to numb their extremities and make them feel too nauseous to cause any trouble. Every thirty minutes a robot that looked like a canister rolled by and stunned them again.

Without wanting to be obvious about it, Beaulieu glanced ahead and counted. Thirty-eight, no, thirty-seven people stood ahead of her. Processing was going very rapidly. Past the access point she could see a decontamination booth. That was standard procedure. But as far as she had been able to determine, no one was coming out. Either they had a different exit point, or . . .

She ducked completing that thought, then felt ashamed of herself. A competent doctor should be able to face anything, no matter how unpleasant. Certainly she had faced death before, in many guises and many forms. She had not always saved her patients, but she had saved enough for her to feel that her existence made a slight difference in this universe.

Battling death was one thing. Standing like tame cattle in a slaughter line was something else. Her courage kept failing her, leaving her with bad moments when her mouth dried out and she could hear her own heartbeat. Then she had to dig her nails into her palms in order not to disgrace herself.

The people in line, wearing Fleet uniforms of gray, now rumpled and stained, were mostly youngsters, lacking enough officers to steady them. They kept glancing back, seeking faces they knew, their eyes darting to hers and away. There was little talking. They smelled death, the way animals do.

Beaulieu had looked up and down the line herself. So far, she had not seen any of her comrades. The only person she knew was Captain Serula, standing fourteen people ahead of her. Serula had not glanced back a single time, and for a while Beaulieu was angry at her. Then she saw Serula's hand clasped tightly by the man in front of her. He was Serula's height but nearly twice as broad, with massive shoulders that strained his uniform. His hair was as dark as Serula's was fair. They stood as close to side by side as the line would allow them. Beaulieu understood. The husband. Dying together was better than dying alone.

Her eyes stung unexpectedly with tears. She'd had a husband once. God, how long ago? Thirty years? For a foolish moment Beaulieu couldn't remember his name. Then it surged back to her. Chaka Narenga of the distinguished College of Physicists. Handsome, brilliant, already famous for his theories of particle dynamics, Chaka had filled her eyes from the first time she saw him. They had spent a year together, complete and happy, he busy with new professorial duties, she finishing her last months of residency. Then she'd gotten the chance to join the Fleet and jumped at it. Chaka went on a tour of research with a team of Minzanese engineers. From that point their paths diverged until they saw each other once every two years, then every five, then there seemed no reason to keep the marriage anymore.

Now, she didn't know where he lived or what he was doing. She could no longer remember clearly what he looked like. She didn't even know why she should be crying over him, except that she needed his passion right now and all she had was a ghost.

Serula and her man went through the decontamination booth. Beaulieu shuffled forward. The robot came back down the line to stun them again. The Boxcan in front of her leaned over and retched miserably. Beaulieu put her hand on his back; it was all the kindness she could offer.

But inside her anger grew. This was no way to go, tame and helpless, unable to fight. She didn't even know *why*.

Two ahead of her. She could see past the decontamination booth now. A door slid open, yawning as dark as a throat. The young Boxcan disappeared.

With a faint sense of shock Beaulieu found herself facing a globe that pulsed white. When it spoke to her, its synthesized voice was flat and impersonal. Somehow that made it easier.

"Name. Species. Age. Gender."

Beaulieu answered these questions.

"Step forward."

She obeyed, thinking even then that she ought to turn and make a run for it. What did it matter if her legs felt like cold molasses? Being shot in the back would be quicker than this.

But she did not want the youngsters around her to misunderstand. She didn't want to be thought a coward.

Proud fool, she thought, and entered the booth.

Gas, smelling of antiseptic, fogged lightly around her. It felt greasy upon her skin. The rear door of the booth opened and she stepped forward into the waiting darkness.

The door closed behind her. She stood there, unable to see and slightly disoriented. Nothing happened. After a moment she drew a breath, feeling as though this whole thing was rather anitclimatic.

A light flashed on, dazzling her so that she shielded her eyes with a forearm.

"Beaulieu, A. Physician. Scientist."

Was that a statement or a question? Beaulieu waited a moment, then said, "Yes."

"Follow the light."

The overhead light moved to her left. Beaulieu frowned but followed it. She stumbled off a ramp and fumbled past a bulkhead through a doorway that slid open jerkily as though seldom used.

The light was small and so tightly focused upon her that it gave her almost no illumination as to where she was going. It remained the only light she had. Sometimes it got too far ahead of her and had to wait, shining down at the floor until she stood beneath it again. At such times she was able to see that she was in a corridor, a very narrow one fitted with circuit boxes and sealed cables.

Her last stun dosage wore off with the exercise. She began to feel better.

"What the hell is going on?" she said softly.

After a few minutes when this trip looked like it was going to go on forever, she stopped, letting the light move on without her. When it finally sensed she wasn't following, it hovered.

"Beaulieu, A. Physician. Scientist."

"Where are you taking me?"

It made no response. She stood where she was. After a moment the light returned to her.

"Follow the light."

It moved away, but Beaulieu did not follow.

"Where are you taking me? I'm not following you until I know that."

The device obviously had limited programming. It returned to her. "Follow the light."

"No."

She had the feeling, however, that this argument could go on forever. Whatever was going on, at least she hadn't been processed yet. Maybe she was being rescued.

Grumbling beneath her breath, she walked forward. The light moved ahead of her, and she gave it no more trouble.

When she began to think she would walk down this dusty, cold corridor for the rest of her life, the light stopped and shone upon a door.

"Place hand upon sensor."

Beaulieu peered at the door and located an oblong panel upon the door. It didn't look like a sensor, but there seemed to be nothing else. She pressed her palm against it. The door slid open, and light from the other side spilled through, engulfing her.

She stepped inside warily and found herself in a gleaming, sterile room all in shades of white and soft gray, fitted with desks, human-contoured chairs, bio-computers, and a library containing rack after rack of hard data.

Siggerson sat in one of the chairs, eating from a bowl of steaming liquid. Ouoji sat on the table beside him, their heads nearly level. She noticed Beaulieu first and her tail twitched a greeting.

Astonished, Beaulieu came forward. "Siggerson, am I dreaming? What are you doing here? What am I doing here? Where are the others? What is this place?"

A tiny spotlight clicked on, shining into her eyes. "Beaulieu, A. Physician. Scientist. Computer will give you all duty assignments. Check them now."

The light clicked off. Beaulieu glared at the ceiling. "I'll do no such—"

"Don't," said Siggerson, only now glancing up from his soup. His eyes were red-rimmed with a strained quality to them that had her reaching instinctively for the medikit that had been taken from her. "Don't resist them. You don't want to be chopped up, do you?"

He spoke in a queer, jerky voice, sounding as though he

couldn't get any air into his lungs. She leaned over to check his pupils, then took his pulse. It was racing.

"What have they done to you? What's wrong with your lungs?"

He shook his head, averting his eyes from hers. "You don't want to know. Just don't cause any trouble."

"Siggerson—"

He gripped her wrist, and his fingers were icy cold. "Don't do it, Beaulieu! You don't want to meet your masters. You don't!"

The hysteria in his voice alarmed her. She held his face in her hands and looked into his eyes, trying to calm him. "All right, Olaf. I won't cause trouble. Just take it easy. Try to take some deep breaths before you hyperventilate."

He coughed, pulling his head free. "Hurts too much. Just leave me alone and do your work."

He needed attention, but Beaulieu could tell that any attempts to take care of him would only agitate him further. She backed off, puzzled and worried. Ouoji crossed the table to butt against her. Beaulieu met her intelligent blue eyes, wishing for once that Ouoji could actually talk.

Ouoji chittered and jumped off the table. She trotted over to the computer and turned to stare at Beaulieu. Her tail lashed once, imperiously.

Sighing, Beaulieu touched the screen to activate it.

"Beaulieu, A.," it said. Words scrolled across the screen and stopped. "Duty assignments for Work Cycle 1. Commence immediately."

Beaulieu read with a deepening sense of outrage. "The hell I will! This is telling me to catalog DNA codes and start cross-matching them with previous entries for duplicates. Whose DNA codes? Those kids back there that I just left?"

"Were you in the processing line?" said Siggerson.

"What is wrong with you? A whole crew just went into the chopper and you—"

"You don't know what these things are," he said with a spark of his old self. "They can make you serve them. Don't make them do that to you. They g-go inside your lungs. They suffocate you. They invade . . . and they—they *force* you—"

His voice broke and he began to cry.

Horrified, Beaulieu stood there and swore at herself for not having realized he'd been tortured. He was still in shock, and she'd blundered around with the finesse of an oleanphatant.

Ouoji ran to him and jumped back onto the table. He clung to her for comfort, and her blue eyes glared at Beaulieu over his head.

"I'm sorry," said Beaulieu. "I was scared back there in the processing line. I thought I was done for and so I've been yelling ever since."

He nodded, his head still bowed away from her. "They need scientists to finish the work," he said, sniffing. "Holborn is in charge. He'll come by soon. It's my rest cycle. I—I don't have to work yet. W-watch what you say. They listen."

Beaulieu started to speak, then realized she couldn't find words adequate enough to express what she was thinking. She went out of the room and found herself in a glass chamber. Fog curled against the three walls. Through its swirling whiteness she could glimpse row after row of drawers. A code bank.

Before her was a panel of switches designed to open selected drawers. A small screen could be used to call up code data and cross-match it with other reference files. All done by remote, with no possibility of breaching the perfect sterility of the bank's environment.

It was an engineering marvel. The scientist within her admired such an efficient setup. The rest of her was appalled. Were Kelly, 41, Phila, and Caesar already in there? What was it all for? What in God's name was going on here?

Then she thought of Siggerson's broken spirit and his

warning that it would happen to her if she didn't comply. There had to be a way out of this.

But in the meantime she had better go to work. It was, at least, a means of searching for the rest of the squad.

Holborn was awakened from his sleep cycle by an insistent buzzing. He raised his head, and the lights came on, showing him he had fallen asleep at his desk. His back and neck felt sore and stiff. He straightened with a groan. The notes and figures upon his desk were meaningless squiggles. He stared at them, moving closer as though proximity would bring understanding. But it remained gibberish. He rubbed his eyes and sighed.

The buzzing continued. Holborn heard it now. With a frown he rose stiffly to his feet and stood hunched like an old man. He knew that noise. That was an experiment-ending alarm. Someone had been careless and forgotten to remove a batch of cultures from the Series G tests.

Angry, Holborn left his office, limping through the area where an unconscious Kelly still lay upon a gurney awaiting pickup for processing, and entered the testing section of the laboratory. Righa lay sprawled upon the floor, his lower limbs drawn up against his abdomen. His mouth was open; his eyes stared sightlessly. He had been dead for some time. Holborn crouched beside him, but he did not touch Righa's scales. The cause of death did not really matter. Righa was a creature of sun and desert. He had never flourished here.

With a grunt of exasperation, Holborn rescued the baked cultures and set them to steaming upon the counter. They stank. He slapped the nearest one to the floor, where it shattered.

"What do you expect from me?" he shouted at the ceiling. "Maon! I must have reliable help! Do you hear?"

His voice echoed in the room. Holborn walked out, crunching upon the broken glass. A robot would come in and clean up the mess.

A carrier stood in his office when he returned. It held no Visci box, however.

Disappointed, Holborn said, "Where's Maon? I want to speak with it."

"Message from Maon: We are finished with processing. Earth studies are completed. Sufficient codes have been collected. Stage Two is ready to commence. Shut down this station and follow carrier to new station."

Holborn stared stupidly at the carrier. His tired brain was conscious of something wrong, but he kept thinking it was simply because he did not understand. "But I haven't finished. I mean, I am close, perhaps within one generation of eliminating the biotoxin. A few more hours—"

"We have seen completion projections. This work can be finished by workers."

Holborn was shocked. Machines in his laboratory, machines observing the final, glorious mutation . . . no.

"It's my work," he insisted. "I have the right to complete it."

"New tasks have been assigned. New assistants are already at work."

Holborn opened his mouth, but no words came out. He flushed to the roots of his hair and his soft white hands clenched at his sides. "Wait," he said, and stepped back out of his office to gain a moment of composure.

There, in the dimly lit privacy, he backed against Kelly's gurney, making it rattle. His whole body was shaking. They couldn't do this to him. He had believed his masters, trusted them. He had endured his fatigue and his fear in order to find the cure. It wasn't fair. They owed him more than this. He was a scientist, after all, a rather famous one in his own time. He couldn't just be shunted to a new task like some hireling.

"Damn you," he whispered. "Damn you!"

Behind him, Kelly moaned. Holborn whirled as though stung. For a moment in his rage he wanted to strike the unconscious man. Kelly had jeered at him and insulted him.

Kelly had implied that Holborn was nothing more than a deluded puppet. Was it so clear that even a stupid soldier could see it?

Holborn felt branded with shame. Kelly hadn't been sent yet for processing because his code was essentially a duplicate of another Kelly already listed among the samples.

"Garbage," muttered Holborn. "Useless garbage. You'll be cleaned up with Righa and the rest of the trash."

"Holborn," said an overhead speaker.

He jumped, his heart racing as though he had been caught doing something wrong.

"Coming," he said.

His voice was oddly breathless. He still had the urge to smash, to destroy. But he was just a doughy, soft specimen, nothing like this man lying here with muscles as hard as iron. A professional soldier could destroy. He would fight if he had the chance. Kelly wanted revenge upon the Visci for what Maon had done to his friend.

Holborn blinked rapidly, going momentarily into a fugue as his brain shut down conscious thought. For several seconds he stood there, staring at nothing. Then he reached out and jerked the catch on Kelly's restraints.

"Holborn," said the speaker.

He came back with a start. Blinking, he stared around and wondered what he had come in here for. He went back inside his office where the carrier awaited him.

"Follow the carrier to your new station," it said. "Duty assignments will be made there for procedure in infecting DNA codes."

Again Holborn felt stupid, as though he were three steps behind. "But that test isn't necessary," he said. "We collected the codes for examination in—"

"Codes will now be infected prior to return to Earth."

"What!"

The carrier came toward Holborn. In his shock he didn't notice.

"You can't do that!" he said. "It's immoral. Tampering will cause mutations—"

The carrier seized Holborn's arms and lifted him bodily. Holborn screamed before he realized the carrier wasn't going to crush him to death. It turned and bore him from the laboratory. He made no further efforts to struggle. And as he grew calmer, his sense returned. He could not make any more protests or he would be terminated. But at the same time anger burned his stomach like acid. His masters were treating him, Ansel Holborn, like a common hireling. After years of brutal effort to save lives, he had been reassigned to a murder team.

He had never been permitted to do any cloning, but he'd seen the facilities within the City. Magnificent, technologically advanced far beyond anything he'd ever seen before. How many codes had he collected? Thousands. Which meant thousands of mutant clones to be released on Earth prior to the Visci invasion.

Oh, he had been a fool, a blind, conceited fool to believe they meant the people of Earth no harm. And being made into a fool was perhaps the worst insult of all.

Holborn blinked, his eyes burning and hot against his eyelids. Small things seemed to be snapping inside him. Each snap *hurt*. He gnawed at the inside of his cheek until he tasted blood. He swallowed it, sampling the coppery taste without any conscious awareness of it.

When the carrier at last put him down at his new station halfway across the City, Holborn walked in meekly ahead of it. He saw two humans, male and female, and some kind of furry creature with blue eyes. His new assistants. Holborn glanced at them, then looked around the work area. It was spotless, well lit for once, and humming with activity. His assistants must already be cataloguing the codes.

"Processing will be finished by the end of this work cycle," said the carrier. "Then all codes will be in place. Carry out assignments."

It left, leaving Holborn alone with the strangers. He resented them, resented their competence, resented the stiff way they were looking at him.

Maon had underestimated him. Maon thought he was too cowed to do anything but obey. But Maon had robbed him of his victory over the plague, and Holborn had already thought of the perfect way to defeat his masters.

"I'm Holborn," he said. "Stop working until I understand my duty assignments. Then I'll coordinate everyone's efforts."

No one answered him, but Holborn didn't notice. He had work to do.

11

Kelly awakened with a start. He tried to sit up before he remembered he was strapped down. But the restraints were loose. He pulled free and snatched the strap off his throat with a vengeance. Like a cat he rolled off the gurney and landed silently upon his feet in a half crouch. He listened, trying to place the noise that had awakened him. But he heard only quiet.

He went right, aware that he didn't dare hesitate long while he had this chance of escape. He found himself in an overheated lab where equipment he couldn't identify hummed busily. A vaguely reptilian creature lay dead upon the floor in the midst of broken glass.

Kelly backed out of there at once. In the other direction he found an office of sorts, littered with papers, data files, and color charts of cell structures. He hurried through without examining anything.

Not until he was outside in the cool gloom of a corridor the size of a street did he pause to wonder who had set him loose. Holborn probably. Kelly wasn't going to waste time thinking about it. He had to find his bearings and locate his people. His instincts were screaming urgency. He had the sense of having slept too long, of having missed something important.

About forty meters along the corridor, he found what he'd been looking for: a hatch to a service passage. It took some time to figure out how to gain access, but once it opened, Kelly was through in a flash. He let out his breath, feeling slightly safer in this narrow place. His presence triggered a sensor of some kind, for dim lights winked on at long intervals. Kelly's hair prickled on the back of his neck. He wondered what else the sensors had registered and relayed. But just the same, he wasn't a robot with headlights built in. He needed the illumination to operate.

A toolbox fitted with probes, scanners, circuit interrupters, and the like proved a treasure trove. He tucked the tools into his pockets, keeping only the circuit interrupter in his hand in case he met something metallic and nasty along the way. Now he didn't feel quite so helpless.

About then he heard footsteps. Kelly froze, his breath locking up in his lungs. He pressed his back to the wall and strained to listen. At first all he got were echoes, then his hearing sorted through them and he determined that they were coming his way from the direction he was heading.

He could reverse direction, but Kelly's stubbornness made him hold his ground.

His heart, however, was jumping erratically. He didn't want to admit he was afraid. But he had to. It could be another damned warbot hunting for him, and he knew he didn't have a prayer against one of those. Still, he didn't run for it.

The footsteps stopped, and that worried Kelly even more. He listened for what seemed like an eternity, aware that he was probably being picked up on a scanner but still unwilling to start making noise until he had to.

He closed his eyes a moment, regulating his breathing and trying to pull himself under control. He realized he was gripping the circuit interrupter too hard and consciously loosened his fingers around it.

Just as his nerves were about to unravel, the footsteps started up again. They were irregular, sometimes rapid, sometimes slow. Kelly frowned. Somehow they didn't seem to belong to a machine.

Eagerness leapt inside him, but he reined himself in. Something alive and fugitive didn't mean it was friendly. He'd seen what the Visci looked like, but there could be other, equally hostile species aboard this city-ship. If it should be one, his circuit interrupter wasn't going to be of much use.

Kelly eased along silently until his shoulder pressed against a small bulkhead rib. That would hide him until X was almost on him. Maybe. He hugged the wall, trying to flatten himself as much as possible.

The footsteps halted again and stayed quiet for so long that Kelly's nerves were screaming by the time X finally started coming. Kelly tensed himself. Just as X came even with him, Kelly sprang, grasping the wrist of X's knife hand and stepping in close to land a couple of hard chops to the throat and ribs while X was still reacting.

He heard a grunt and grasped a thatch of wiry hair. Kelly brought up his knee as he pulled X's head down. There was a satisfying thud and X sagged. The knife clattered upon the floor. Kelly hobbled back, his knee aching, and looked for the knife. He couldn't find it in the gloom.

His quarry lay facedown on the floor, but Kelly had already determined he was human. Cautiously he knelt, wishing the light were better, and reached through the gloom for X's shoulder. X, however, snaked out an arm and grabbed Kelly by the throat, heaving him over in a fierce roll to his back. Suddenly, not quite sure how it had happened, Kelly found himself on the bottom and X on top. X was throttling him. Kelly thrashed and did his best to pry X's fingers off his throat. His ears roared; the gloom began to swim around him. Kelly brought up the circuit interrupter to X's carotid and zapped him with it.

It was a low voltage current and couldn't do much harm, but it startled X. His grip loosened, and Kelly kicked him in the stomach, thrusting him back. Kelly scrambled up, heaving for breath. His throat felt like mashed gristle.

"Now, you blob-lover, try some of this—"

"Boss!"

Just in time Kelly held his punch. He blinked in the gloom, trying to see X's face. But he didn't have to. Only one person in the galaxy called him that.

"Caesar?"

"Yeah!"

Caesar loomed close and gripped his shoulders with a gleeful shake. "Yusus, you nearly scared me to death, jumping out of the dark like that! You okay? I thought by now you were probably chopped liver."

"Almost," said Kelly. He massaged his aching throat. "That was the sloppiest Kramer flip I've ever seen executed."

"Worked, didn't it? Caught you like a flat."

"Yes," said Kelly ruefully, "it did."

"I'd like my prong back," said Caesar.

Kelly crouched at once and began to feel along the floor. "It slid out of sight down here somewhere."

Caesar knelt and searched with him. "Got it! You could have rimmed out my guts at one point. Instead you tried to electrocute me."

Kelly showed him the circuit interrupter. "I was cleaned out, prong and all. This was all I could find. You want a probe?"

"No, but Phila will."

"Phila! How many of the others have you found?"

"Zip," said Caesar. "Phila and I were caged together. She got us out of that little playhouse, and so far we've figured out the teleport grids and part of how this place is laid out. Most of it is dock pods and hangars. There's a vast central control area. Then everything else is storage and labs."

"Good work."

Caesar shrugged. "Phila's the one who plugged into the central system and got all the information. Not that she's brilliant or anything. It took her a while to get the hang of binary. She nearly brought down the emergency seal bulkheads at first. And there are a lot of surveillance tabs. It's a very suspicious system. She has to keep exiting every few seconds and finding another route of communication in."

"So where is she?"

Caesar jerked his thumb over his shoulder. "Back that way. She says the prisoner holding pens are this way, the way you came from. I was going to reconnoiter."

"I don't like leaving her on her own," said Kelly. "I want us to stick together. Let's go get her. Then we'll find the others."

"Yo."

Getting to his feet, Caesar took the lead along the service corridor.

"We got loose. You got loose. You know something? I don't think these robots are all that smart. I mean, they're armed, some of them, and they have surveillance all over the place. But they don't seem to have any AI in their programming. So it's not that hard to step around them if you have to. Also, in the main corridors you're likely to run into some that have been switched off. Like they don't have a job to do at the moment and have been shut down to conserve energy or something."

"Makes sense," said Kelly.

"Yo, but it gives me the creepilworts. This whole place has nothing but machines rolling around in it. Makes you wonder who built it, a race of machines?"

"The machines have masters," said Kelly grimly.

"But where? Is this place run by remote control, or what?"

"No, the Visci are on board. Have you seen any robots carrying boxes?"

"What kind of box?" said Caesar, glancing back.

Kelly gestured with his hands to indicate size. Caesar nodded.

"Once. So?"

"So a Visci was inside. They're something between a liquid and a gas. The robots carry them around and speak for them."

"And they feel like warm pudding."

Kelly frowned. "What's that? You've encountered one?"

"Sort of. We didn't know what it was and we didn't stop to chat. Not exactly candidates for the Alliance standard of beauty, are they?"

Kelly didn't feel like joking. "No. You were lucky. I watched one kill 41."

"What? You serious?" Caesar turned around and stopped. His face was a pale blur in the gloom. "41's dead?"

"Yes. The Visci smothered him. It was deliberate, cold-blooded murder."

"Yusus," said Caesar softly. "I always figured old 41 had as many lives as a cat. I—I'm sorry, boss."

Kelly nodded and looked away, his throat working. As soon as he could manage his voice, he said, "They intend to invade Earth and take it over as their new home planet. Some kind of plague is killing them where they come from."

"Now that's just too bad. They can go squat on somebody else's world."

Kelly grasped Caesar's shoulder. "We're going to stop them. Whatever it takes, their plan ends here."

Caesar's gaze met his. "I get you, boss. Will do."

The translation system reported unauthorized queries coming through the lines, but no trace back had as yet been accomplished. Maon applied the proper pressure and eyes opened. It remained difficult to adjust to seeing through such distorted vision, requiring reflected light, inversion, and binocular coordination. Periphery was limited, making it necessary to turn the head in order to scan. Even then, head movement was limited, making it necessary to turn the entire body in order to scan completely.

Long ago, it had been a mark of great strength to ride a Svetzin. Before age and before the plague. Now, it was harder to maintain control. And some of the patterns were different than memory told, bringing puzzlement and sometimes confusion. Had Svetzin changed so much? Evolved so quickly? There was no longer a bifold lobe at the rear of the brain to grasp. Without its centralization, control was made more difficult, for separate centers of the brain had to be located and pressured.

Sensory impressions had also changed. Too many scents proved a distraction. This Svetzin did not seem as strong as its ancestors. Heart raced blood too fast, upsetting brain patterns with excessive oxidation. Lungs had voluntary and involuntary muscles in the way of humans, making control harder. Muscle spasms also distracted. This Svetzin was a fighter. Once Maon would have relished the challenge; now it made an annoyance.

But the freedom from a carrier created great satisfaction. Freedom from that box, that prison, even for the short while this body could remain alive was worth all annoyance and effort. Soon, there would be an end to all dependence, and the Visci could be free in the oceans of Earth.

Soon. Soon.

Maon gave the command, and right hand touched a control. A screen lit, and eyes absorbed information.

"Unauthorized data transfer routed to repair unit 1101010 in service corridor 000011."

The translator took the command straight into binary: "Seek and cancel data transfer."

Cancellation came at once. Maon watched intently. Seconds later a new unauthorized data transfer began. The trace reported a different line of use. Maon canceled it.

Seconds later data transfer began again. Again on a different line.

Maon considered this. A deeper trace went out, checking all the lines of use, and Maon discovered the data transfer still originated at the same repair unit. An intelligence was manipulating the simple programming of the library computer.

Maon stood and turned the body about. Two carriers waited nearby with siblings Suol and Kaen. Maon dispatched a trio of fighters to catch the intelligence and identify it.

Speak Maon: "If human, it will bear out my theories on the resourcefulness of this species."

Speak Suol: "We disagree. Humans are not the threat you consider."

Speak Kaen: "They are parasites. Weak. Unaware of us. They would make useful servants and should remain upon the planet."

Speak Maon: "They must be destroyed. We have observed their capacity for resistance."

Speak Suol: "Why have they been captured so easily? Their behavior pattern shows they have limited experience with superior life forms. Once frightened by immersion contact, they serve without resistance."

Speak Kaen: "They are not significant from the other species that we have observed with them."

Speak Maon: "They are devious and stubborn. They resist the idea of serving. Even frightened, they will resist. We could never trust them. Much energy would be wasted watching them. They must be destroyed. I have guided the work of Holborn. His antidote for our affliction will in turn become the biotoxin that will destroy humans. The retrovirus injected into the DNA code of these samples—"

Maon's translator overrode it, sending an alert in rapid binary. The intelligence had escaped. The fighters required instructions.

Maon gave a search and locate command and returned to the discussion with its siblings.

Speak Suol: "You live in the past. Dreams of old greatness, even dreams of riding lesser beings such as this body you inhabit. There is danger in this practice. We are beyond bodies."

Anger touched Maon. It almost broke the speech pattern by saying, "Then why do we need them so much?" but it waited for Kaen's turn.

Speak Kaen: "Agreed. It is unwise to go so far without your carrier and habitation."

Speak Maon: "Prison! I hate the box!"

Speak Suol: "Discipline yourself, sibling. Our task is greater than personal emotion. We have searched time for generations; now our task is soon accomplished. Nothing must jeopardize our victory."

Speak Kaen: "Agreed."

Speak Maon: "I have not lost the task. I have ever kept it before me. It is foolish to accuse me of less just because I see need for eliminating the humans. Our plan will go forward. No changes from the program I have set. Agreed?"

Silence.

In its rage Maon lost partial control, and the body went into spasms.

Two. Separate. I am—
One!

Maon regained control, but the spasms continued in a light series, irritating Maon who was not ready to surrender this ride so soon. Only a Svetzin was strong enough to be ridden, and in this time there were no more Svetzin besides this one unit. It must endure longer.

Speak Maon: "Agreed?"

Speak Suol reluctantly: "Agreed."

But Kaen did not speak. Its carrier bore it away.

Maon let it go. Kaen had fertilized and was close to reproducing. Kaen had never been very reliable. Had it not threatened the triad of family, Maon would have wished Kaen to go inert.

Suol's carrier brought it closer. Disapproval from Suol's thoughts touched Maon, but Suol had not leave to speak in the broken pattern, and Maon did not reestablish a new one. Maon needed its attention elsewhere, for there was much to be done before launch.

Kelly held his breath and squirmed deeper into the cavity beneath the floor. Above him a warbot clumped back and forth in a search pattern. Its scanner must be fairly primitive or else its instructions were incomplete. Obviously it had found Kelly for it kept circling over his hiding place, but it seemed not to know what else to do.

Kelly, however, wanted its weaponry. Clutching the circuit interrupter in a sweaty hand, Kelly eased his legs up beneath him. From this angle he could see a jack bolt on the right heel of the warbot, for recharging. That's what he had to hit with the interrupter.

Small target. One chance.

He swallowed, his heart beating hard. In his mind he tried to stay loose, not put too much pressure on himself, not lock up.

It was turning, walking away. Wait . . . wait . . . *now*.

He came up in a surge, his arm and shoulder hitting the floor grille and knocking it open with a crash. He was just centimeters away from the warbot's heel. It turned at the torso and aimed at him. Kelly jammed the interrupter upon the jack bolt.

Blue fire sizzled around his hand. The warbot froze in that twisted position, its right weapon still aimed at Kelly. Its headlights went out.

Relief swamped Kelly. He scrambled out of the hole and made a kick jump at the warbot, sending it toppling with a crash that would probably bring a whole squadron of rusty buckets coming. Using the probe, Kelly opened its torso plate and swiftly disconnected the power pack before it could switch over to auxiliary batteries and reactivate the warbot. He swiveled off the left forearm, which was really a plasma launcher. Tucking the power pack under his arm, he hooked up the launcher and was in business.

Wasting no more time, he starting running up the service corridor.

Caesar was sixty meters ahead of Kelly and in trouble. The plan had been to split up in hopes that a warbot would follow each of them. The first had gone after Kelly. But the remaining two stayed on Caesar's tail, ignoring Phila. Now that was discrimination, if he ever saw it. What was this, pick on men and leave women alone day?

He had barely managed to scramble up here into the ceiling struts where cables and loose wiring tangled everywhere. He figured they wouldn't shoot so freely where there was a chance of damaging circuitry. But his little scoot up the access ladder hadn't been quite fast enough to avoid getting one leg scorched pretty badly. It hurt enough to make him cry out, and cold chills of shock kept running through him, throwing off his concentration.

So here he was, one little ape up on the monkey bars, and it took only·one slip or one grab of a non-insulated cable to say bye-bye to Mrs. Samms' red-haired boy.

He had his prong and a probe. Neither was much good against a pair of black, metallic giants with blasters for hands. But even giants had their weak spot. He stared bleakly down at the tops of their heads and wondered what it was.

Kelly had said be quiet, not alert the whole place to what was going on. But, hell, these tin cans had shot first. One of them now aimed upward with extreme care. Caesar could see the muzzle dilating down to a small aperture, which meant the warbot intended to fry him between the eyes with a millimeter-thin beam of plasma.

"Not so dumb after all," muttered Caesar, and scrambled precariously among the struts to a new perch.

The warbots shifted ponderously beneath him, scanning. Caesar opened his tunic and peeled a skin bandage off his rib cage. He had to bite back a yelp. It had been on there too long and it took a little hide with it. But the slim, finger-length capsule looked just as new as the day he'd stolen it from the munitions lab back on Station 4. He'd kept it all this time, afraid to use it because nitrax-5 was as dangerous as a sun going nova. It wasn't in usage yet because the lab boys couldn't figure out how to make it safe for the user. Caesar had itched to have one, just one capsule, simply because it existed. He'd seen the demo tapes of its tests. It made a contained explosion, small in radius compared to its power. Beautiful. If set off inside a metal container, it expanded the metal, then contracted it so the box had a tiny, crumpled appearance. Very neat.

But another demo tape showed that the same-size capsule blew the same-size metal container to such micro bits that the whole lab rained ash. That was the tape that had to be edited to remove footage of the technician who left a few body parts lying around.

Caesar swallowed hard, beginning to sweat. A fifty-fifty chance at best. Who knew what age did to this little bomb? Who cared? He couldn't wait.

The warbots had positioned him and were aiming again. One fired, and Caesar yelped as the plasma beam sliced through the strut he was perching on. It gave beneath him, and he jumped clumsily to another, raking his injured leg through wiring as he went.

"Try this, you—"

He flipped the switch on the side and threw the bomb straight down. There was a sickly greenish orange flash of light, topped by a roar of fiery heat that came mushrooming straight up. Caesar couldn't run, couldn't move in time. There was nowhere to go except where the concussion of the blast threw him. And that was a long, long way indeed.

12

The blast shook the corridor and a wave of heat and debris came belching toward Kelly. He dived to his stomach. Coughing, he buried his face until it rolled past him. Then he got to his feet and hurried forward through the settling dust. What in the five galaxies had Caesar done?

He found himself crunching over small bits of robot almost before he realized it. The corridor walls were buckled. A severed power cable snaked about, crackling dangerously. Flames flickered on what remained of the ceiling.

The actual area of destruction wasn't that large, but it was thorough. The explosive gel Caesar was so fond of hadn't done this. Maybe one of the warbots had exploded. Kelly frowned, kicking a metal foot out of his way. No chance of salvaging these bots for weapons.

And there was no chance that this would pass unnoticed.

A short distance ahead the access hatch slammed open. Kelly dropped to a crouch, aiming his launcher.

Just in time, however, he recognized Phila's dark curly

head and held his fire. With her came the shrill whoop of an alert siren.

"Commander!" she said breathlessly, slamming the hatch and cutting off the sound of the siren. "We've got to get out of here fast! It sounds like the whole army is converging on this spot."

"Where's Caesar?"

She blinked. "Isn't he with you? I thought the pair of you pulled this off."

"No. When we split, I had one bot to deal with and I saw the others heading after the two of you."

"They went after Caesar, not me," said Phila. She held a blowtorch jacked into a power pack belted around her hips.

"The bots are here. Where's Caesar?"

They exchanged a look, and a cold feeling of dread went through Kelly. Not another one, he thought.

Swiftly he moved on along the corridor, knowing there had to be something left. Phila trotted behind him.

"We have to hurry. We can't stay here. Commander!"

Kelly ignored her. Part of the ceiling had come down in a long spill of wires, twisted metal support struts, and shattered panels. Kelly sorted through them quickly. Phila helped.

It was she who found Caesar. She crouched quickly, not speaking. Kelly noticed her stillness and came scrambling through the debris to her side.

Caesar lay on his stomach, twisted and still, his face hidden. Dust had powdered his hair. Kelly put a gentle hand upon his shoulder, slid it around to Caesar's throat, found a faint pulse.

Kelly withdrew his hand in surprise. "He's still alive. Quick. Help me get him out."

Together they shifted a ceiling panel to one side. An access hatch slammed open somewhere back along the way they'd come. Kelly and Phila exchanged a single glance, then Kelly disconnected his launcher and exchanged it for Phila's blowtorch.

"Cover us while I pull him free."

"Right." Phila jacked in the launcher, her small hands handling it deftly as she checked charge levels and twisted the trigger wires around her forefinger. "Get going. I'll be right on your tail."

Kelly hoisted Caesar over his shoulder in a fireman's lift and hurried heavy-footed along the corridor. Pursuit sounded awfully close. Then he heard the roar of Phila's launcher engaging. He risked a glance back and saw her standing straddle-legged in the center of the narrow corridor, squeezing off controlled, short bursts in a pattern that kept her shielded.

She couldn't hold that position for long, although the warbots would be hampered by their size in the small space available. After a few minutes Kelly heard a check and shift and knew she was falling back.

Come on, Phila. Don't be too big a hero.

Footsteps came pounding after him. Kelly lit his blow-torch, finding it a pitiably inadequate weapon if he had to take on plasma launchers. It came to life with a pop and the acrid smell of burning gas. A faint trail of blue flame burned at the end. He waited until he got around a bend in the corridor, then turned, putting his back to the wall. Caesar felt like a metric ton, hampering him. His breath was already coming pretty short.

But it was only Phila racing after him. She took in his defense stance with a single look and kept going without missing step.

"I've stopped them temporarily by melting a couple of bots together across the corridor, but that won't hold long."

A heavy crashing noise in the distance punctuated her words. Phila glanced back, her black hair tossed half across her face. Kelly caught just a glimpse of her eyes, wide with a touch of fear but intent in the way of an animal on the hunt. His squad had never panicked yet, no matter how bad the situation around them. He'd chosen them well.

"It's not far to the lab where Beaulieu and Siggerson have

been assigned," she said. "I think we ought to leave the corridor now and double back with the teleport to confuse their scanners. How are you doing with Caesar?"

Ceasar wasn't a big man, but he was stocky and solid with muscle. Kelly didn't waste breath by answering her question. He waved her on. Both of them knew he wouldn't abandon Caesar, no matter what.

She crouched at the next access hatch, listened a moment, then eased it open. Kelly knelt there, easing Caesar down. The front of Caesar's uniform was charred and bloody. Kelly checked Caesar's pulse and found it fast and thready. Not good. Phila peered outside, slid through, and fired her launcher.

Following, Kelly was in time to see the warbot's head go tumbling, sliced neatly off. Confused, the bot circled. Kelly dashed after it and jammed the circuit interrupter against the jack bolt on its heel. It thrashed a second, then shut down. Kelly pulled out his probe, and Phila joined him in opening the bot's torso plate. She worked like lightning, disconnecting the power pack quicker than Kelly could. He unscrewed both firing arms this time and Phila finished converting them to manual use by the time Kelly dragged Caesar through the hatch, wincing at how rough he had to be.

"Sorry," he muttered. To his relief, Caesar remained unconscious. His face, however, looked pale and waxy. Kelly got him over his shoulder and stood, balancing carefully.

A monitor floating on a small anti-grav unit came into sight. Phila shot it to bits and rolled the bot over so she could open its back panel. She plucked out several metal throwing stars, gingerly handling their sharp edges, and a hand weapon.

"It probably has a lot more gadgets tucked away."

"No time," said Kelly. "Let's move."

She nodded and headed left. "This way. There's a teleportation grid at every intersection of the corridors. All the levels are labeled according to a binary code. So it's very easy to identify where you're going. Just follow a logical progression."

They hit a ground-eating trot, the siren wailing in their ears.

"Surveillance cameras?" asked Kelly.

"I shorted them out in this section," said Phila with a grin. "Doesn't mean they don't have plenty of other nasty little surprises."

She stepped onto a scarlet grid set into the floor. Kelly joined her, watching while she touched the setting she desired on a control box. With a rather dramatic flash of light, they entered displacement and came out again almost in the space of one heartbeat.

They could have found a contingent of warbots waiting for them. Instead a trio of canister-shaped robots ringed the grid. Flexible tubing with nozzles on the end swung in their direction. Kelly took half a dose of the stun before he managed to slag one. Phila dealt with the other two.

A siren went off, and Kelly cursed.

"So—so much for doubling back." He stepped off the grid and nearly fell as his knees sagged.

Phila steadied him. "How much of that did you get?"

Kelly shook his head, wanting to be sick, yet knowing he wouldn't be. Stuns were always the same, noxious and uncomfortable. But he wasn't hurt, and he could still function.

"Go," he said. "Forget the fancy stuff. Just get us to the lab. Caesar needs help, and you need a computer. We can do more damage by direct access to the system than by slagging everything in sight."

"Affirmative."

They hit a trot, Kelly weaving like a drunk, and managed to surprise another trio of warbots. Kelly and Phila slagged them quickly.

"Slow reaction times," said Kelly, unwilling to believe they were being so successful. "Why?"

"Limited programming?" suggested Phila, doing another

sabotage although she was almost overloaded with weaponry now. "They aren't aware that we're armed. We have the advantage until they get updated commands."

Another advantage. Kelly filed it away. Machines were only as limited as their programming. Without AI design, they could not match the ingenuity of humans. But he had not forgotten who controlled these machines. So far he didn't know the thinking patterns of the Visci, but he was willing to bet a year's pay that they had grown too dependent on their machine servants. There was something to be used in that.

Phila pointed. "See that door? I think that's the lab we're looking for."

Kelly smiled at her. "Let's hope your sense of direction has held."

She took the lead, overriding the simple external lock in a matter of seconds. The thick door slid silently open and Kelly heard Beaulieu's voice lifted angrily: "I don't give a triple damn for your duty assignments. I'm not letting you alter these codes by a single—"

"Everyone, freeze!" ordered Phila. She entered fast, covering the room with her launcher.

Coming in right on her heels, Kelly hit the control that shut the door and locked it. He spotted a surveillance cam overhead and shot it.

The sound of his weapon galvanized the room's occupants into action. Beaulieu came shoving past Holborn.

"You're alive! My God, I can't believe it. Siggerson, look!"

Behind her, a wan Siggerson rose unsteadily to his feet and managed a smile. Ouoji leapt off his desk and butted her head against Kelly's knee. Then she reared up on her hind legs and patted Caesar's head with a gentle paw. Her blue eyes met Kelly's.

"I don't know," he said. "Doctor, Caesar's in a bad way."

"Damn." Beaulieu broke from hugging Phila, weapons

and all, and came at once. She bent to peer at Caesar's face, peeling open one eye, then tapped Kelly briskly on the arm. "There's a bunk this way. I don't know what I can do without—"

Breaking off, she turned on Holborn, who had slunk into a corner and stood there hugging his arms. "You! I need medical equipment. Where's the infirmary on this ship?"

He was staring into space and appeared not to hear her. She glanced back at Kelly and tapped her temple.

"Yes," said Holborn without looking at her. "There isn't one. No care. Why we died. Righa is dead now. I—I saw him."

Kelly had a mental reminder of the reptilian alien lying on the floor of the other lab. "Doctor, do what you can."

She waved at an open doorway and started opening storage bins. As Kelly carried Caesar through and lowered him onto a narrow bunk, he heard Beaulieu muttering, "Do something. What the hell can I do without a scanner, a wound sealant, and coagulant capsules?"

She walked into the room and elbowed Kelly out of the way. She carried a hand-operated suction pump of the sort used to clean test equipment, a roll of fabric adhesive, and a bottle of antiseptic.

"You just became a surgical nurse," she said, shoving the things into Kelly's hands. "Turn that blowtorch off, will you? You don't need it in here."

Kelly glanced through the doorway and saw that Phila had already stacked her weapons collection on the desk and was busy at a computer station. Siggerson stood at her shoulder.

"We don't have much time until we're traced here," he said.

"You worry about the time," said Beaulieu. "I'll worry about this boy."

Taking a lab knife, she cut away Caesar's blood-soaked tunic. She drew in her breath sharply enough to confirm what Kelly already suspected. But she didn't speak, just went to work quickly, her hands sure and gentle. With the suction pump she cleaned Caesar's chest until the actual wound itself was exposed.

"Puncture to the left lung. Has he been bubbling?"

Kelly frowned. "I didn't notice."

"At a guess I'll say it missed his heart. Not by much though. He's in shock. Lost too much blood. Spongy here. Crushed ribs. Hand me the adhesive."

Kelly obeyed. "What's that for?"

"I'm going to bind him up." She tore the center from a clean lab smock and folded it into a pad. "Hold that on the wound. Light pressure. Yes."

Kelly could feel Caesar's blood soaking through the cloth. It was warm against his fingers. He frowned, warding off a sudden onslaught of dizziness. *Pretend you don't know him. Pretend that's not his life running out under your hand.* Beaulieu wound the tape around Caesar's chest, binding him up tightly.

"Good. Ease him down now." She checked Caesar's pulse, frowned, and examined the rest of him, shaking her head over the burns she found on his leg. "I can't do much for this. Let's let him rest a bit."

She turned away to wipe her hands on what remained of the smock. "He's lucky I took a class once in antique medicine methods. Our ancestors used to rely on little more than bandages. I guess we can too."

Kelly wasn't so sure. "He's still bleeding."

"Not as much. Some of it is drainage. Looks worse than it is." Her eyes lifted to Kelly's. "But he is one hurt boy. He shouldn't be moved, and as soon as possible he has got to have proper care."

Kelly nodded, but not to agree. "We can't stay here. The whole ship is on alert. It's only a matter of time until we're traced here. We've got to locate as many of the prisoners as we can and get—"

"Kelly. They're here."

At first he didn't understand. Beaulieu led him away from Caesar's side and said, "Go on through. In there."

She pointed. Kelly stared at her a moment, then walked into a glass bubble surrounded by white fog. A computer screen glowed with a list of names. Kelly leaned past it, pressing his face to the glass.

He saw row after row of drawers.

"It's a genetic bank, the finest I've ever seen," said Beaulieu behind him. "Every conceivable variation of DNA combinations has probably been collected and stored in there."

Kelly pulled back, unwilling to consider the horror of the idea yet forcing himself to. There wasn't time for shock or for denials.

"You're saying the crews of those missing ships are here?"

"Their DNA codes, yes. And several other species as well, including some of the long-extinct Svetzin. It's a treasure trove, Kelly. Something that scientists should—"

Kelly turned sharply to face her. "Everyone? Including my father?"

Beaulieu's eyes softened with compassion he did not want. "Yes," she said softly. "I've been going through the names. My assignment was to—"

Kelly stopped listening. He felt as though a wedge had been driven through his chest, making it almost impossible to breathe. "Those bastards," he whispered. "Not my father too."

"Kelly—"

He turned away from her and smashed his fist into the glass partition. Little crazed stars radiated through the glass from the point of impact, but it did not shatter. His fist felt numb, then as he pulled it back, pain flared hot through his knuckles.

It wasn't supposed to happen this way. Victor Randolph Kelly had too much vitality, too much worth as a human being to end up part of a butterfly collection in someone's vault.

He drew back his fist to smash the glass again, and all the while the wedge in his chest was working its way into his throat, trying to throttle him. A faint voice, the admiral's voice, ran through the back of his mind: "If you can't keep your temper, son, if you can't make your anger work for you in bad situations, you'll never be able to think of a way to solve them."

But, Dad, he wanted to say, *this isn't just a bad situation. It's* . . .

He didn't strike the glass again, just leaned against it so that the cool, slick surface of the glass pressed his burning cheek.

"Kelly," Beaulieu was saying. "Kelly, *listen*. We can get them back. They can be cloned. They aren't lost completely."

Her words registered, bringing a sharp surge of hope. Kelly straightened and looked at her, then he frowned.

"Clones. Physical duplicates. But no minds."

"Well, the mind would be there. Just a blank slate. They would have to be reeducated. That's not impossible."

Kelly thought of his father, of the admiral's forty years of experience, of the brilliant tactician who was as much a product of his mistakes and triumphs as of his education. Kelly shook his head. "You could fill him up with knowledge, but not wisdom. You could tell him what his wife looks like and who his children are, but he wouldn't remember the day Drew won his first soccer tournament or when we dared J. J. to ride a pholox and she broke both her wrists falling off. No, Doctor. It couldn't be the same."

"No," she agreed sadly. "But you'd have a piece of him. And that's better than nothing."

"Is it? I'm not so sure."

Kelly turned away, not wanting to discuss it further. He thought of the starships waiting in the hangar and his plan to sail them out of here. Their crews would never travel the stars again. He stared at the drawers, mentally saying goodbye.

And how would he face his mother and his brother and sisters, assuming he got out of here in one piece? What would he say to them? Sorry, everyone, but I failed.

Their faces blurred and he closed his eyes tightly.

The admiral . . . 41 . . . maybe Caesar, if they didn't get out of here soon.

Kelly opened his eyes, blinking the tears away. He left the control bubble, refusing to look back.

Phila and Siggerson both glanced up when he came in. "How's Caesar?" asked Phila.

"Hanging on."

She frowned worriedly. Kelly's gaze slid past her a moment to Siggerson. He looked unwell, shocked somehow. His hands were unsteady, and it seemed an effort for him to concentrate on the smallest things. Kelly's determination slid. Without Siggerson, their chances of getting home got even slimmer.

"Here's the whole layout, Commander," said Phila, calling up a diagram onto her screen.

Kelly bent over her shoulder to study it. She changed it to cross-sections, close up.

"We're here, fairly close to central control. Beyond it lie a series of connecting docking pods."

Kelly straightened, possibilities running through his mind. He knew that even if they managed to sneak on board a ship, they had a very small chance of actually getting away. There was the time jump to make, and the danger of leading their pursuers right into populated space.

"I've put some jammers into communications through these sections here." She pointed. "All the machines are on binary, and that's the easiest language to screw up. Depending on which ship you want to take, I might even be able to communicate with it from here, getting its automateds warming at least. Siggerson says he can—"

"Do it," said Kelly. "Pick the ship you want, Mr. Siggerson."

The pilot shivered. "I . . . don't know. Without the correct coordinates, we can't navigate back. At least, I don't think I can."

"You don't think?" said Kelly sharply. "I don't want opinions, mister. I want solutions. They are all heavy class. Are you able to handle a destroyer or a battle cruiser?"

Siggerson blinked helplessly. His eyes were lost. "I—"

"Dammit, man! Shape up! 41 is dead and Caesar is in there dying now. If we don't pull together on this fast, we'll all be done for!"

Siggerson covered his face with his hands, and Kelly shook him. "What the hell is wrong with you?"

"Kelly!" said Beaulieu from the doorway. "Don't. He can't help it."

"Yes, he can," said Kelly. "He's a Special Operations officer."

Siggerson's hands dropped from his face. From the corner Holborn came forward.

"You haven't communicated with the masters," he said. "Remember your friend and the way Maon touched him?"

Holborn's glassy face and his bloodshot eyes held madness.

Kelly scowled at him. "I can hardly forget it."

Holborn gestured at Siggerson. "This one has been touched also. As I was. It is a way to show us who is master."

Kelly whirled to stare at Siggerson in consternation. "One of those things went inside you?"

"Kelly, go easy," said Beaulieu, but Kelly wasn't listening.

His gaze bored into Siggerson, who slowly nodded. Tremors went through Siggerson, and the effort for him to meet Kelly's eyes was visible but he did it.

"It—it was like suffocating. It was in my lungs. I

couldn't breathe. I thought it was going to kill me. But it came into my mind also. I—I couldn't keep it out."

Siggerson looked away. His hands shook so violently he clenched them at his sides and still they shook.

Kelly swallowed. He didn't know what to say. Gently he put his hand on Siggerson's bony shoulder and gripped it in apology. Then he glanced at Holborn.

"41? Any chance of—"

"That touch was not momentary," said Holborn. "You saw."

Yes, he'd seen. Kelly hadn't even allowed himself to hope. Not really.

"It isn't enough just to get out of here," he said to all of them. "We have to stop the Visci from invading Earth."

"Yes," said Holborn. "They want to send the clones in among the population and infect them with a plague."

"There's a cloning vat on board this ship?" asked Beaulieu.

"Extensive facilities," said Holborn with pride. "I helped refine them. I—"

"They're here, on this level," said Phila, pointing at the diagram.

"Never mind that," said Kelly. "Holborn, how do we stop them? Once and for all?"

Holborn stared at the floor for several seconds. When he looked up his face was red and his eyes wild. "There are many aboard. Hundreds of thousands. Perhaps a million. They are in the containers that you have seen. Almost in an inert state. Some, no doubt, have become totally inert in all this time. The City has been here a very long time, seeking answers to the plague that is killing them on their home world. The City was built originally to create a sterile, safe environment for them. But most do not dare venture out from their containers."

"And?" prompted Kelly impatiently.

Holborn pointed at an isolated section on Phila's diagram. "They are in this place. Most of them. Cut the seals, break their environment, and release bacteria from my laboratory. They will die."

Phila and Beaulieu exchanged glances. Siggerson straightened his shoulders.

"I'll help do it," he said.

"Murder of helpless civilians?" said Beaulieu very softly. When Kelly glanced her way, her eyes were like obsidian. His own blue ones hardened in return.

"I'll get the biotoxin," said Holborn eagerly.

He started out, but Kelly blocked his path. "No."

"Oh," said Holborn with a blink. "You mean it is not safe to venture out without protection. May I have a weapon?"

"No."

Holborn looked at him and read something in Kelly's face that made him pale. "You're not going to do it? Why? Why? We must kill them. They'll conquer us if we don't. They'll—"

"Without the robots they are helpless," said Kelly. "Phila, you've got to tap into central control."

"It's guarded. They'll trace any interference right to us."

"Take the risk," said Kelly. "Unless you can tap into the main systems, you'll never be able to shut the whole place down. Siggerson and I are going to try a physical assault on central."

Siggerson's face took on a little life. He went to the weapons pile and began sorting through them.

"Excuse me, Commander," said Phila. "But we've got to have something better than those two approaches in order to breach that area. The forcefields will block you, and—"

"All right. Show me a detail of the area."

Phila's diagram changed. Kelly studied the circular area carefully, noting the approaches and the way it was fitted into the curve of the hangar. A couple of entrances in. Easily defended. Phila was right. He frowned, then traced his finger down a service corridor.

"What's this?" he said, pointing at a small box of a room.

"Generator, major power supply."

"We'll take that out," said Kelly.

"Auxiliary will replace it."

"But there will be lag time," said Kelly. "That's our chance."

"Yes, sir, but look. It's not a regular passageway like the others. It's not even a half meter in diameter. Too small for any of us to get through."

Ouoji jumped onto the desk and chittered loudly.

"No," said Siggerson in alarm. "Not you."

But Kelly stared deep into Ouoji's eyes and smiled. "All right," he said. "But you must be very careful."

Ouoji raised her ear flaps in the equivalent of a shrug. She got in Phila's lap and stared at the screen.

"Show her the route, Phila," said Kelly. "I'll rig up something."

Holborn said, "But that's an animal. You can't seriously expect—"

"Ouoji is *not* an animal!" said Siggerson hotly, sounding more like himself with every passing minute. "You must be a xenophobic idiot. Now shut up and stay out of our way until you're needed. I'm not even sure we ought to trust you as far as we can throw you."

Holborn backed off.

Smiling to himself, Kelly knelt at the weapons pile. After a few minutes he had rigged together a small harness and clipped a probe and his trusty circuit interrupter to it. Ouoji let him fasten the harness around her, her silky fur tickling his face as she wriggled closer.

"Now," said Kelly while she stared intently at him. He showed her the probe and explained how to use it to loosen rivets to open a panel.

Ouoji curled her paw around it, holding it awkwardly. Kelly wasn't sure she could handle it, especially since she lacked an opposable thumb, but Ouoji was intent upon what she was doing. She experimented with the probe, dropping it, then picking it up between her digits. That worked better and she chittered approvingly to herself. Using her paws and teeth, she managed even to clip it to her harness.

Her bright blue eyes met Kelly's and he gathered her up in his arms. "You're wonderful," he said. "The other tool should be pressed against . . . can you show her a picture of that, Phila?"

Phila patiently explained the procedure to Ouoji, telling her what to touch and what to avoid. Kelly joined Siggerson and fitted himself with a power pack and two launchers, plus some of the throwing stars. He gave the hand weapon to Phila.

She grinned. "I'd rather have the blowtorch."

"I'll leave that too." Kelly pressed her shoulder. "You and the doctor watch yourselves. And don't trust Holborn."

She glanced at the scientist. "Right. Luck, Commander."

"May we all get home again." Kelly boosted Ouoji up and put her into a service vent. "You too, Ouoji. Do your job and get back here."

By way of an answer, she managed to flip her furry tail under his nose as she scrambled into the vent.

Kelly headed for the door, Siggerson following. Without scanners, there was no way of knowing what might be waiting for them outside.

Kelly hit the control and the massive door slid open. The corridor looked clear. He ducked out and started running with Siggerson close on his heels.

Just before the door closed, Holborn slipped out and was gone before Phila could grab him.

"Hey!" She swore and hit the door with her fist. "Damn!"

Beaulieu came. "What's wrong?"

"Holborn. That snake is gone."

"Do you think he went with Kelly?"

Phila shook her head. "Who knows? If he did, the commander will have his guts for garters. If he didn't, then we're all in trouble. I figure he's gone to blab everything."

"I figure you're right," said Beaulieu slowly. "Can we warn Kelly?"

"How? No communicators, remember?" Phila kicked a chair out of her way. "I was supposed to keep an eye on the little *konard* and I—"

"You can throw your temper tantrum later," said Beaulieu coldly. "We're safe in here. They won't dare jeopardize the codes."

"Safe? Yeah," said Phila sarcastically. "And what's going to stop them from gassing us the same way they did when we first arrived?"

A flush darkened Beaulieu's cheeks. "Of course. I'd forgotten that. I guess we can't—"

"Yes, we can!"

"How?"

Phila's stomach tightened at what had occurred to her, but she nodded to herself. "The commander won't like it."

"The commander," said Beaulieu dryly, "tends to want to clap the women and children under the hatches. Endearing in an old-fashioned way, but impractical."

"What was the name of their leader? Mup?"

"Maon."

"Check." Phila seated herself at the computer station, where her infiltration program was still running, seeking every available spot to play havoc with the systems. It wasn't having much success.

She opened a direct communications line, overriding binary transit. "This is Operative Mohatsa calling Maon. Operative Mohatsa calling Maon. Hey, if you hear me, you'd better answer. We've got your DNA code collection, and we're wondering whether to trash it. You want to talk this over?"

Then she sat back and grinned at Beaulieu. "How's that for an opening bluff?"

"You'd better hope he doesn't call it," said Beaulieu with a serious frown. "Those codes are too precious to jeopardize—"

Infuriated, Phila jumped up. "Look! You can define life down to tachyons if you want, but to me those aren't people in there. They're just some cells—"

"They can be cloned back to life!"

"To hell with that," said Phila. "Our first priority is defending ourselves. The commander expects us to hold this position."

Beaulieu stared at her. "Do you realize Kelly's father is one of those samples?"

Phila felt as though she'd been punched in the stomach. She glared at Beaulieu. "So I promise not to break his petri dish."

Beaulieu's angry retort was cut off by the familiar sound of hissing. They both looked up, and Phila pointed at the pale gas coming in through a nozzle.

"Quick," she said, and hurried into the control bubble. She unsealed the access lock and waded through the misty cold that condensed on her skin. Her hand grasped a random drawer and pulled it open.

Inside, her conscience was twisting inside her, telling her this was like going on a rampage through a nursery. Beaulieu *was* right. Life was life, no matter how few the number of cells. Phila hesitated, cursing herself and the whole situation. This was an officer call. She wasn't trained for a command decision, one involving other lives.

But these were Fleet personnel, not civilians. They'd taken an oath of service that said they would die if necessary to protect . . .

She choked and looked back through the glass wall where Beaulieu stood. The doctor was clutching her throat, beginning to collapse. Was defeat and the subsequent invasion that would bring an end to Earth worth one person's conscience? Phila's eyes blurred with tears that froze on her cheeks. She put her hand inside the drawer and pulled out a handful of codes carefully preserved inside protected slides.

"God forgive me," she said, and flung them on the floor.

She stamped them, feeling a part of her sicken and die inside. The tears ran freely down her cheeks, but she reached inside the drawer and pulled out more slides.

An alarm went off over her, flashing frantically, sending its message back to central control.

She threw the slides on the floor and reached for more when Beaulieu gripped her arms and stopped her.

"Enough. Enough," said Beaulieu. "The gas has stopped."

Phila straightened, unable to turn around and face the doctor. She was sobbing. She had to cling to the drawer for support.

Beaulieu hugged her gently. "Come on. Leave them on the floor. Most of them are still intact. Come on."

Phila let herself be taken out, but once the chamber was resealed, she dashed the tears from her face. Defiance was all she had to cover her deep shame.

"So now I'm a murderer," she said angrily. "I've killed before, dammit."

Beaulieu faced her watchfully, without expression. She didn't have to make any accusations. Phila had plenty for herself.

"It had to be done," said Phila. "They have to believe we'll do anything to stop them. They have to think we don't care; otherwise we don't stand a chance. To hell with it."

Phila walked back to her computer, passing Caesar, who looked so small and still and bloodied her heart ached with fresh worry. They were in bad trouble here. They really didn't have a prayer of getting out, even with a commander as good as Kelly. Hope sagged from her.

But there was training to cling to, training that said a Hawk never gave up until the mission was accomplished.

Do I really believe that shit? she asked herself.

She felt lost, as though her whole belief system had crashed. Then from somewhere deep came the certainty that she *did* believe it, had to believe it. Had to stand for her people, her kind, her species. Otherwise someone bigger and meaner and more ruthless came in and took over. It was the law she'd learned in her childhood on a rough, uncivilized colony world. It still applied.

She dried her face and made her hands stop shaking. Then she opened a line to Maon.

"Hey," she said, using the cocky street tones of her home world. "Maon, you listening to me? It's time we cut a deal."

This time she got a direct reply. "I hear you, Mohatsa. Do you wish to serve us?"

What a laugh. But she started talking, knowing that as long as she kept Maon distracted, Kelly had a much better chance of succeeding.

13

Holborn scuttled along the corridors, veering and stumbling and chuckling softly to himself. This was his chance, his one perfect chance. He would show them, his great, indifferent masters, that he wasn't just a servile worm to be used and then discarded.

He found his former laboratory more by instinct than by any conscious seeking. The lights came on. He looked around, seeing nothing changed, nothing touched. His breath sobbed in his chest. He wiped the perspiration from his face with unsteady hands. Tears of joy ran down his cheeks. Now, now, now was the time to do it, the perfect time, while Maon was occupied with defeating Kelly's attack.

Holborn laughed, rubbing his hands. He staggered to the vault. It took him three tries to unlock it. He kept forgetting the sequence, and his hands were unsteady. But at last the massive door slid open with a faint hiss of released air. A cold, stale odor rolled out over him. Breathing deeply of it, Holborn drew himself fully erect and entered.

He opened one of four chests and from the ice inside withdrew a tiny vial of amber liquid. Death, here in his hand. Safe enough at this temperature, but let it warm to a mere 4 degrees Celsius . . .

His fingers curled around it, thawing it against the warmth of his own flesh.

Chuckling, he left the vault standing wide open and made his way to the forbidden part of the City. It might take him a couple of entire work cycles to walk there, but that did not matter.

Overcome the pain, these grooves of pain, these firebrands of agony.

Overcome the oneness. Break it. Make the oneness two halves.

Separate. Apart. Independent.

Two. We are two. I am . . .

No! Oneness!

Kelly and Siggerson almost reached central control when they rounded a bend in the corridor and came face-to-face with a motionless phalanx of twenty-seven warbots standing three across and nine deep.

Kelly's gut did a flopover, and Siggerson let out a small, strangled sound. But Kelly didn't hesitate.

"Open fire," he said, and triggered both plasma launchers.

He slagged the first row, taking out their weapons in his first sweep, then cutting them at the knees, so that they sagged, melting slowly together. Siggerson took out the second row, thus fouling the return fire from the third. Warbots struggled forward, trying to climb the heap of scrap metal smoking in their way. Their clumsiness was almost comical, except for the deadly blast of a plasma bolt that passed so close between Kelly and Siggerson that the sleeve of Kelly's uniform charred.

"Fall back!" said Kelly, and they scrambled back around the bend of the corridor.

Siggerson was bone-white, and Kelly couldn't quite get his breath. They were badly outnumbered. He needed to think, dammit, think.

His gaze rose to the exposed struts of the ceiling framework. He elbowed Siggerson and pointed.

"Up. Move it!"

The swiveling action of a surveillance camera caught the corner of Kelly's eye. He swung and blasted it. By then Siggerson was up the ladder rungs bolted to the wall. Kelly started up them just as the warbots came around the corner.

Hooking his elbow over a rung, Kelly grabbed one of his throwing stars and flung it at the nearest bot. The star sliced cleanly through gleaming hull metal, and a shower of sparks erupted from the bot's throat. It veered crazily to one side, fouling the path of another. Siggerson slagged them both from above, giving Kelly time to finish climbing up.

Balancing on the struts while maneuvering around wasn't easy. Kelly got tangled in wires and nearly panicked before he extricated himself. But after the first hectic moments, he got the hang of it: move forward, fire, move, fire, move again. As long as he and Siggerson kept to random movement patterns the bots below had trouble tracking them. Whatever kind of warfare the bots had been designed for, it wasn't guerrilla.

The last one aimed right at Siggerson and fired before Kelly could slag it. The metal strut supporting Siggerson sheered. He made an effort to spring to safety but fell, dragging a light track and wiring down with him in a sparking, crashing mess.

"Siggerson!"

Frantic, Kelly watched him fall. Dust fogged everywhere. Kelly swore to himself and hunted for a way down. He skimmed down the ladder rungs and clambered recklessly over a fallen bot hot enough to scorch the soles of his boots.

"Siggerson," he said, kicking the debris away and going again through all the horror he'd felt when he found Caesar. "Olaf, are you—"

Siggerson sat up, coughing. "Just . . . wind . . . knocked out of me," he said.

Kelly helped him to his feet and dusted him off. A camera ahead of them swiveled their way. Kelly blasted it. It was really a waste of plasma since Maon knew they were coming, but Kelly hated the things.

"Let's go. I'm fine," said Siggerson, although they were already walking.

But Kelly moved away from him to the opposite side of the corridor and got both hands on his launcher triggers. A forcefield slammed up just centimeters away from him. Kelly halted, unable to keep from glancing uneasily over his shoulder. Sure enough, a forcefield went up behind them. They were neatly trapped.

"What now? Is this it?" asked Siggerson, still out of breath.

But Kelly remembered how Caesar and Phila had escaped. He didn't have a prong but he did have another throwing star. Pulling it out, he knelt at the beam set and began prying gingerly.

Siggerson touched his shoulder. "Let me do that. You're going to electrocute yourself."

Kelly moved out of the way. Seconds later blue fire crackled everywhere, making him cringe. The field ahead of them fell. They ran forward.

Nothing else came at them. Kelly didn't like it, however. There had to be more. It couldn't be this easy, just two defense postures to overcome.

He felt it before he saw it. A crawly, creepy, crackling sensation that sucked across his skin and made his hair stand up in swift prickles. Kelly halted, frowning.

Siggerson took a couple of steps on, then he too halted. He threw out his hand in warning.

"Look!"

Kelly squinted ahead, but the corridor as usual was poorly lit. He couldn't see anything more than the fact that an intersection lay ahead.

"What is it?" he said. He ran his tongue across his teeth. They were itchy. His skin felt like it was shifting around on his bones. He backed up a step in spite of himself.

"An open teleport beam," said Siggerson.

The unconcealed fear in his voice affected Kelly. They used teleportation all the time, but it was never something you could take for granted even with all the safety features built in. And rule number one was to never, never, never leave a beam open. He'd heard horror stories of people getting sucked into it and either being sent nowhere or coming out reassembled into pathetic things that quickly died.

"We must not go closer," said Siggerson.

"I'm not arguing," said Kelly. Mentally he ran back through the layout. Even if they doubled back and tried the other route in, there was no guarantee they wouldn't run into this same thing. "But just how close can we get?"

"No!" said Siggerson firmly. He shook his head at Kelly. "No closer. Do you know what happens if you—"

"Yes. But we can't just stand here." Kelly frowned and looked back the way they'd come. He looked at the ceiling. "Could we go over it?"

"No. Too close. It's not passive, Kelly. Even from here, I can feel its pull."

Kelly knew Siggerson wasn't exaggerating, but something had to be done. He slung the launchers over his shoulders out of his way. "I'm going to try," he said grimly.

Siggerson gripped his arm. "Don't be a fool! You can't make it. To even try is suicide."

"And what other alternative do we have?" retorted Kelly. "We can't wait on the very slim chance that Ouoji will knock out the power plant. Something is going to come along here very soon to collect us. And I won't turn back and accept defeat. I just won't."

He stared into Siggerson's eyes. Reluctantly Siggerson released his arm and moved out of the way.

His dour expression gave Kelly no confidence, but it had to be attempted. He climbed up into the ceiling struts and began carefully crawling forward.

Before he'd gone very far, he could feel an insidious pull that made his skin feel as though it were being turned inside out. He squinted his eyes to protect them. Tingles went through his teeth until he found himself grinding them fiercely and forced himself to stop. He paused, gasping, and all he wanted to do was go back.

But he'd already made his decision. He forced himself on. Now he was close enough to see the grid. It glowed with a pulsing light that filled the corridor with an eerie luminescence.

What had only seemed to be a pull now became a powerful sucking force that drew first his feet, yanking him half off his perch. His stomach folded over a crosspiece, and he tightened his grip desperately. His launchers slid off his shoulders and dangled from his elbows, getting in the way. He could feel the drag increasing, as though the machine sensed it had him. His fingers loosened despite his struggles to hang on.

When his right hand came off, it was a shock. He flailed and slid, coming to a wrenching halt that jarred him to the shoulder. His left hand clung with a death grip. The rest of him dangled above the grid.

He gasped for breath and tried to pull himself up far enough to grasp the bar with his right hand. His fingertips brushed it and slid away. Grunting with the effort, he tried again and didn't reach as far. Perspiration ran into his eyes, stinging them. He tried a third time, telling himself he *could* make it.

Instead, he slipped. His left hand gave out, and in that last split second of awareness, he knew he was falling straight onto the grid, straight into nowhere, never to return.

14

It didn't happen.

One moment he was falling. The next instant he hit solid metal, flat on his back, with a jarring impact that made him think he'd broken in half.

He lay there stunned in total darkness, with all the wind knocked from him.

Siggerson snapped on a torch and came running. "Ouoji did it! She did it! Kelly, you idiot, I thought you were done for. Some people have all the luck. I can't believe her precise timing."

Kelly couldn't either. He tried to answer, but without any wind all he could do was make a strangled noise. Siggerson dragged him up to a sitting position, too excited to even check for broken bones, and thumped him enthusiastically.

"Come on! We've got to move before they realize what's going on. There will only be a few minutes before the auxiliary plants activate to divert power here from the other generators."

Kelly sucked in some air and began to feel like he might

live. His arms and legs moved. It looked like all he had were some bruises. Lucky was right. He felt profoundly grateful to Ouoji.

Together they headed along the corridor. Siggerson's torch beam stabbed here and there, giving them glimpses of doors half open. Two carrier robots each holding a Visci box stood immobile as though their communications-directions line had been broken by the power shutdown. Kelly and Siggerson eased cautiously past them and hurried on. The dark silence was creepy.

It seemed also empty. They passed three warbots, all immobile, frozen in midstep.

"I told you," said Kelly. "Without their robots and power to run them, the Visci are helpless."

They stepped through the half-open doorway at the end of the corridor and Siggerson shone his light around.

It was a spacious, circular chamber. On the far side a vast expanse of glass overlooked the hangar. Everywhere else stood silent banks of instrumentation. Even in the intermittent stabs of illumination from Siggerson's torch, the technology's sophistication was evident.

"To have this," breathed Siggerson. "To be able to take even a part of this home. Do you realize just what kind of engineering geniuses they are? This whole ship the size of a city . . . how do they power it? The genetics labs. The interdimensional travel—"

"Just don't forget what they are and what they want," said Kelly grimly. He took a few steps forward, paused, and looked around.

The silence was almost audible.

"Well," he said. "Looks like this is our chance to—"

"I saw something!"

Kelly spun around. "Where?"

Siggerson's torch flashed. "There. No, it's moved. Damn!"

Kelly turned, scanning the whole shadowy room with his finger on the trigger. The darkness pressed upon him like a living thing. He could feel a menacing presence he hadn't detected before, a malevolence that made the muscles tense in his shoulders.

The torch went out. Siggerson shook it, but to no avail.

"No," he said, his voice shrill. "No! It has to work! It has to—"

"Siggerson," said Kelly sharply. "Forget the torch. Get your weapon ready and put your back against mine. Now."

Siggerson complied, his breathing audible and jerky. Somewhere in the darkness around them, a Visci waited for its chance. Kelly swallowed, remembering how 41 had died. He imagined one of the things crawling up him to his face, smothering him, going in . . .

His heart jumped. He wiped his sweaty face, trying to get rid of the images in his mind.

A low hum made him flinch. An array of instrumentation lights came on, then the overhead lights returned, dazzling them.

Kelly blinked and squinted. From the corner of his eye he saw a tall shape nearby. He whirled, his launcher ready, and just in time held its fire.

"41," he said, his voice hollow with disbelief. "41?"

Dammit, he had *seen* the man die. Yet here he stood with the lights gleaming upon his long tangle of blond hair. His tawny eyes stared at Kelly with the flatness of no recognition. He was breathing. His gaze shifted from Kelly to Siggerson, who lowered his weapon.

"Thank God, it's only you, 41. I wasn't sure what we were about to face in here. Kelly, I thought you said he was dead."

"I thought he was," said Kelly. He looked at 41, wanting to feel glad, wanting to feel relief. But something was wrong. He couldn't place it, but the Visci had done something to 41 and left him . . . "How do you feel? At the first chance, we'd better have Beaulieu take a look at you. Where is—"

41 looked away and flipped a switch. A synthesized

voice came through a speaker: "I am Maon. I ride this body."

Siggerson backed away, but Kelly frowned and went toward 41. Closer, he could see the signs of physical distress: a sheen of sweat over pallid skin, dilated eyes, irregular breathing.

"Come no closer," said Maon.

"You must release him," said Kelly. "We aren't beasts of burden for your use. You're killing him!"

"That does not matter. To ride is a sign of strength."

"And who are you trying to impress? Where's your audience, Maon?" Kelly swept his arm around to indicate the empty control room. "You don't impress us."

"You are nothing."

"Wrong," said Kelly. He aimed one of his launchers at a control panel and pulled the trigger. An arc of plasma spanned the distance and slagged it, sending sparks shooting.

41 turned fast, nearly lost his balance, and barely caught himself.

"No!" said Maon's voice. "Fool, you must not destroy—"

"Release my friend," said Kelly. "Look, Maon. We don't have to be enemies. I know about the plague that is killing your kind. I know that you need another planet to settle upon until the plague is cleaned out. But you don't have to conquer us just to save yourselves. Together, using all our resources, we could find a solution."

41 stood motionless for a long moment until Kelly thought Maon might be going to relent. Then 41 reached out and pushed a rapid series of controls. Nothing happened at first, and Kelly suspected it might be a call for help.

"Kelly!" said Siggerson.

Hearing the despair in his voice, Kelly turned just as the muffled rumble of an explosion shook the windows. Lights had come on inside the hangar. Kelly ran to the glass and looked out at the nearest destroyer. The explosion had crumpled her bridge and engine areas. He could see the crumpled hull quite clearly. Another explosion shook the windows. Another destroyer disabled. Another. And so on in rapid succession until not one ship remained untouched.

Kelly watched helplessly. Their avenue home was now closed. He should have felt as sick with despair as Siggerson looked, but instead all he knew was anger, harsh and corrosive, fueling his determination.

He turned back to Maon.

"Your defiance is futile," said Maon. "Your actions have made little difference. You accomplish nothing against us. How can you fight us? We are your superiors."

"No," said Kelly. "I don't think you are. I think you are scared and desperate, used to overwhelming other cultures with your advanced technology, and too savage to know what compassion means."

"We do not subscribe to the lesser emotions. And we are not desperate. We shall overcome the plague as we overcome all of our problems. Already an antidote has been discovered. You, trapped inside a physical shape that is large and clumsy, are far too primitive to—"

"Too primitive for what?" broke in Kelly. "To run our own worlds? To shape our own destiny free of your interference? To resist you? To help you? If that's true, why did you need a human researcher to find the antidote for you? Why do you need clones of humans to conquer Earth for you? Why not just go in there yourself? You have the ships, the weaponry to defeat us. Or do you?"

"We have ships," said Maon sharply. "Many."

"Then dispatch them."

41 made no move. His tawny eyes stared into space, eerie and remote as though he had no cognizance at all of what was happening. Could he survive this? Or was Maon in him to stay?

"You do not order us," said Maon at last.

His delay in answering and the feebleness of his reply caught Kelly's attention.

"Is that all you have to say? Why not start your invasion

now? We have defied you, angered you. Punish us and launch."

Still 41 did not move.

"Who pilots your ships?" asked Kelly. "Robots or Visci?"

Maon did not reply.

Kelly stepped closer. "The Visci are stored on board this ship, aren't they? Locked up in sterile containers to keep them safe. Is that any way to live?"

"Soon we shall be free again," said Maon. "We shall roam the oceans of Earth once it is made safe for us."

"I don't think so," said Kelly. "How many years have you been here? Eventually the robots will wear out. Then what happens? How many Visci have died inside those containers? How many remain alive? Do you know?"

"You mock our agony!" cried Maon. "You are an ignorant savage!"

"How many, Maon?"

"One triad is all that is necessary to regenerate our—"

"Where's your triad, Maon? Those two containers that I saw being carried down the corridor, are they the rest of your triad? Why aren't they with you?"

A green light across the room started blinking furiously. 41 staggered forward to it as though Maon had forgotten Kelly's existence. Kelly joined him.

"What is it? What's wrong?"

"The chambers . . ." whispered Maon. "Not the chambers."

Kelly looked around at Siggerson. "Can you determine what's happening?"

Siggerson slung his weapon and activated a surveillance screen. After a few moments he said, "Kelly, look."

Kelly came over. The screen showed row after row of compartments containing Visci boxes. Thousands of them stretched past counting. Nothing looked wrong, yet the alarm still flashed.

Kelly frowned. "Is the whole race aboard?"

"Yes!" said Maon. "All! We are the City. Our home world is contaminated past reclaiming. Originally we were to be a colony, then we became the only ones remaining. We have searched the galaxy. We have searched time, seeking when we should claim our new home. It takes time, you see, to change the pH balance of the oceans to the proper level. Your seas are full of salt, teeming with competitive life. Without destroying everything, much time is needed to make the necessary alterations. We lack that time. That is why we use interdimensional travel."

"Why?" asked Kelly. "Is there a limit to how long you can live inside the containers?"

"Yes. What have you done to us? Why have you breached the seal of the chambers?"

Kelly and Siggerson exchanged glances. There could be only one explanation.

"Holborn," said Kelly. "He wanted to take the plague to you. I told him not to."

"He must have gotten past Mohatsa," said Siggerson.

"An easy explanation!" shouted Maon. "Easy to put the blame on Holborn, who cannot make a defense. Holborn is a fool, weak and easily controlled. Holborn would not seek our destruction. But you, you are another matter. Already we have seen your kind's attitude toward life. You do not hold your own species dear. Why should you seek to preserve ours?"

"What are you talking about?" demanded Kelly.

41 staggered to the surveillance screen and played back the episode of Phila within the code storage facility, shouting defiance and throwing the contents of a drawer onto the floor. Kelly barely watched it, for 41 had slumped against the control panel. His eyes were sunken, his face yellow-gray. Kelly touched his arm, steadying him. Was 41's mind still intact? Had Maon taken control of it, or destroyed it? 41's face was slack. Kelly could find no spark in his eyes.

"You see?" said Maon as Phila began to weep and

Beaulieu supported her out of range of the camera. "No respect. No understanding of these codes, of their entirety, of their beauty. Our bio-engineering techniques surpass anything you could know. We have cloning facilities here in the City that can resurrect any of these codes. In a matter of hours the tissue is regrown, the thoughts, memories, brain patterns, all is restored as it was before. And yet this unit Mohatsa treats it as dirt, to be bargained with, to be destroyed if necessary.

"Your kind have no understanding of what is compassion. You speak the word, Kelly. You accuse us of lacking in it. Look to yourselves."

Kelly drew a deep breath. "She was crying. She did not enjoy what she had to do."

"Enjoy? Is that a prerequisite for an action? Is justice enjoyable? We debate with you, yet you are too primitive to understand the issues. You think a little; therefore, you believe yourselves great. Unless an alien species evolves along a branch similar to your own, you cannot comprehend it. Unless there are legs and hands, you have no communication with it. We are a thing of horror to you, Kelly. You are shamed by that."

"It is not you, but what you do," said Kelly. "Manipulating us, reducing us to smears of DNA, stealing bodies to be hosts for your own pride, robbing us of our own world. We judge by actions. Yours tell us we cannot trust you."

"And *your* actions? Obliterating an entire species? Will you know how to code our DNA, to save us from extinction? We have our way. We have the right to exist."

"Yes, you do," said Kelly. "But—"

A scream interrupted him. Startled, Kelly glanced over his shoulder in time to see Holborn come staggering into the control center. The scientist's smock was torn and filthy. Blood trickled down his face from a cut over his left eye. His lips were drawn back, baring his teeth in a horrifying parody of a smile. He was quite mad.

Siggerson moved to intercept him, but Holborn knocked him aside with unexpected strength.

"Going to kill them all!" he said, panting.

Kelly grabbed him. "Holborn! Holborn, you've done it. Stop now. Stop."

Holborn sagged in his arms, weeping with pathetic little snuffles. "Slaved for them. Honored to help them. Wanted the glory, you see? Wanted the glory. They wouldn't let me finish my work. Wouldn't let me . . ."

He wasn't making much sense to Kelly. Over his head Kelly nodded to Siggerson. "Help me get him into that chair."

"This wretched unit is defective," said Maon.

At the sound of its voice Holborn jerked upright, getting past Kelly and Siggerson. He rushed at 41 before they could stop him.

"Dead. You're dead. Dead thing. All dead. Have to stay dead."

He threw the contents of a vial in 41's face before Kelly and Siggerson managed to drag him back. But Holborn had stopped struggling now. He threw back his head and laughed with a hysteric note of triumph that made Kelly shove him angrily away.

Kelly went to 41, who was standing there vacantly. The brownish liquid dripped from his cheek onto the collar of his tunic. Kelly held him by the arms, not sure what it would do to him.

41 shuddered in Kelly's grasp.

"My . . . container!" said Maon. "I am too far. I must have it. Must have it!"

"Siggerson," said Kelly beneath Maon's frenzied shouting. "Get Beaulieu here. On the double."

41 sagged suddenly like a limp rag, going to the floor before Kelly could catch him.

"Help me," said Maon. "I want to live. Help me, unit. Help me live."

41 shuddered again, and Maon began to emerge from

him, seeping out from eyes and ears and nostrils. Where
Maon's dark edge touched 41's wet cheek, it shriveled and
withdrew.

Faintly in the back of Kelly's mind, almost as a whisper
of imagination, he heard a scream. Instinct made him drop
41's hand and suddenly back away.

"Stay close!" said Maon's synthesized voice. "Stay close
to me."

Holborn was still laughing. Siggerson and Kelly exchanged glances, then Siggerson aimed his launcher.

"No!" said Kelly. "Not while it's still on 41."

Maon flowed to 41's chest and pooled there. 41 stirred,
as though coming around, then he went into convulsions,
hemorrhaging from his nostrils and ears. Kelly wanted to
rush to him, help him, but Maon waited like a hunter
watching its quarry, and Kelly dared go no closer.

Footsteps came running. Beaulieu said breathlessly, "I'm
here."

Holborn lunged at her, and Kelly intercepted him just in
time. A swift chop to the throat felled Holborn, and Kelly
gripped Beaulieu's arm.

"Quickly. 41 is still—"

A shout from Siggerson made them both turn. Maon was
moving, flowing incredibly fast over the floor toward
Siggerson, who was backing up frantically, knocking over a
chair, and shouting.

"Siggerson!" shouted Kelly. "Shoot it!"

But Siggerson was still backing up, too panicked to
remember the weapon in his hand. Kelly aimed at Maon and
fired. Plasma engulfed Maon, who stopped. But as soon as
Kelly stopped firing, Maon flowed forward again. It was
almost to Siggerson's boots.

Screaming, Siggerson fired on it now, with no effect. He
was pinned against the controls. Frantically he climbed up
onto them and crawled over the boards, shooting again and
again at Maon although it did no good.

Beaulieu moved past Kelly. "I've got to check 41."

Kelly seized her wrist and held her in place. "Not yet."

"Kelly! He could be dying."

She wrenched free and knelt beside 41. Maon had flowed halfway up onto the controls, but now it abruptly reversed direction, falling to the floor again with a soft plop, and headed for Beaulieu.

"Doctor!" yelled Kelly.

She glanced up and tried to scramble out of the way, but Maon moved too quickly for her. It flowed up her boot, and she slapped at it.

"Don't touch it! " yelled Kelly. "It will get to your face that much more quickly."

Even as he spoke, Kelly was moving. He snatched the empty vial off the floor and grabbed the back of Beaulieu's tunic with his other hand, holding her against him as he thrust the vial right to the edge of Maon.

Maon stopped at Beaulieu's hip.

"It will not affect me," said the synthesized voice from the speaker. "I am too strong."

Kelly held the vial where it was, wishing to God he knew how long it took before the biotoxin had any effect. Minutes, hours, days, months? His hand was so close to Maon he could almost feel it. Goose bumps broke out along Kelly's arms, but he did not move. Held in the circle of his arm, Beaulieu remained frozen. She scarcely breathed.

"I can halve myself," said Maon. "Enter both of you. Holborn is a stupid unit. This was not the plague. It does not affect me."

Maon moved, sliding over the vial and Kelly's hand. Kelly felt a warm slickness upon his skin that left it tingling unpleasantly. Maon parted, half flowing up Kelly's arm to his shoulder, then to his throat, the other half flowing up Beaulieu's torso.

Kelly gritted his teeth shut and closed his eyes. He tried to tear Maon from his throat, but his fingers could get no purchase. They slid through Maon and could not grasp it. Kelly jerked away from Beaulieu, hoping that if Maon were

completely parted, that would weaken it. He heard Beaulieu
scream and felt the warm slickness sliding across his lips,
dribbling through despite all his efforts to keep them
clamped shut, forcing them apart.

His eyes flew open in horror. It was going down his
throat, choking him. More of it went up his nose. He tore at
his face, trying to breathe, trying to get it off.

Then Maon stopped. Kelly dropped to his knees and
retched, spitting out the creature. The taste was unspeak-
able. He felt that he could never be clean again. Maon lay
inert upon the floor, small puddles of it splattered between
Kelly and Beaulieu. She was crying, holding herself and
rocking back and forth.

Siggerson slid hesitantly off his perch and went to her.
She clung to him, sobbing harder. Kelly had no such
release. He met Siggerson's gaze, met the sympathy and
understanding there, and began to shiver.

It was only revulsion, physical shock, and reaction. He
let the spasms go on without trying to stop them. In a
storage bin he found a scoop and scraped Maon off the
floor. Scoop and its contents went into disposal. Only then
did Kelly give way to knees too shaky to support him. He
sat down on the floor, thinking about how close it had been,
knowing that if Maon had ever gotten completely into him
he couldn't have stood it, not for an instant.

Siggerson had been touched and he had survived. 41 had
lived with that thing in him for hours. Whether he would
survive remained unanswered.

"You okay, Commander?" asked Siggerson after a long
while.

Kelly nodded. He sat there, drained and spent.

"Looks like we got them all, the damned dirty things. I'm
glad we got them."

"Yeah," said Kelly. "Maon was right."

"About what?"

"We can't make contact yet with a species like the Visci,
a species that different, that alien. We aren't ready."

"Good," said Beaulieu, choking and wiping tears from her face. "I'm glad we aren't ready. I don't ever want to meet anything like that again. If I do, I'll know I've lived too long. We can't coexist with them. We *can't*."

"No, we can't," said Kelly softly.

"Anyway, they're dead," said Siggerson. "Dead and gone. Good riddance, I say."

"Yeah," said Kelly.

But there was no cheering.

15

After some long hours of reprogramming by Phila and Siggerson, the robots worked for them. Records showed that the City had not moved from her current position for at least half a century, perhaps more. The question remained now: could she be moved at all?

Kelly settled himself at his station in central control. Seats had been rigged up for them; robots didn't need seats. These were not comfortable. The controls were spaced at the wrong intervals. There were many that were marked off limits simply because Siggerson could not figure out what they were for.

Siggerson had argued that they should try to rewire the attack ships docked in the hangar area beside the ruined Alliance ships. But they were totally robot ships, not designed for living pilots at all. It just wasn't practical to use them, but Kelly was bringing them along for scientists to study. This whole massive ship would jump Alliance technology ahead by years.

If they could move her. *If* they could navigate her. *If* they could make the proper interdimensional jump to get them home.

Siggerson had lost weight. But he seemed completely absorbed in his work and showed less and less strain from his experiences. As for Phila, there were dark circles beneath her eyes and she was unusually subdued. But Kelly knew she was still dwelling on her actions in the genetics lab. He had tried to talk to her, but she evaded the subject. Kelly worried. He'd gone through this himself, over and over, and he'd seen plenty of his fellow officers go through it. In time she would work through it on her own and come to grips with it, or it would fester and ruin her.

Flashes of binary came in over myriad communications lines as robots and automatic functions reported in. Kelly couldn't translate fast enough. He stopped trying. At this point the bots could report what they wanted; the City was moving, ready or not.

A beep sounded, startling him from his reverie. He flipped a toggle to open a voice line.

"Beaulieu to control."

"Control, Kelly speaking. How're they doing, Doc?"

"Everything's as ready as I can get it. The vats look like they're designed for movement so I've gone ahead and started the cloning process with batch number one."

Kelly frowned. He had not forbidden Beaulieu to clone the DNA codes, but he remained skeptical.

"Yes," he said impatiently. "I meant Caesar and 41."

Caesar remained dangerously weak without benefit of life support facilities. Because Beaulieu would not let Caesar be moved for any reason, it had been necessary to strip down a sick bay from one of the destroyers and transfer the equipment to the genetics lab. Kelly had helped her, leaving Phila and Siggerson to get on with the even larger job of preparing the City for flight. Robots had transported the heavy stuff, but Kelly had been faced with wiring it into a not always compatible power system. The work had been made even harder by a restrained Holborn gibbering insanely to himself and 41's presence—wide awake, eyes staring vacantly, responding to none of the wide range of stimuli Beaulieu tested upon him.

"Yes," she said. "Now that I've finally got something besides a dull knife and a tom-tom to work with, I can report Caesar safely stabilized. I'm feeding him a transfusion right now, and I've been able to seal the incision in his lung. He'll do."

Kelly smiled tiredly. Even Phila and Siggerson looked up with interest. "That's great, Doctor. And 41?"

She hesitated so long Kelly's hopes went plummeting again.

"Well," said Beaulieu finally. "I put the neural scanner on him, and there's less actual damage than I suspected at first. The hemorrhaging looked worse than it really was."

"That's good, isn't it?"

"Kelly, he's retreated psychologically. There are some very good therapy units on Station 4 and even better ones on Station 1, but I'm not sure anyone will ever be able to reach him. His psych profile has always been unsure. That, plus his catalepsy, puts him pretty deep. Beyond hypno-scan and certainly beyond probes, which I think would just make him worse."

"What about a Salukan mind sieve?" asked Kelly.

"Maybe," but her voice was doubtful. "I'm sorry. That's the best I can offer right now."

Kelly sighed. "Thank you. I'll let you know when we're ready."

"Standing by."

Kelly broke the line with a frown. Restlessly he got to his feet and paced around. Siggerson, ever careful, was running a last series of systems checks. Phila called them off for him. She sounded tired. Kelly rubbed his eyes, longing for more sleep than the two hours he'd snatched somewhere. They all needed rest.

But they all wanted to get home.

Kelly paused at the observation port and stared out at the

stars. Familiar stars shining upon a time he did not belong in. By Siggerson's calculations if they simply went back to Earth, they would be two thousand years in her past. It was almost tempting to see what the sixth century was like firsthand.

"The Dark Ages," he muttered aloud.

Phila glanced up. "What was that?"

Kelly came away from the port. "Are we ready?"

"Almost," said Siggerson. Ouoji wandered in and curled up beneath his chair. She smelled of singed fur and unguent. "Just one last simulation. Won't take but thirty-eight seconds."

"Fine," said Kelly. "*Then* we start, Mr. Siggerson."

Siggerson's eyes met his. Siggerson looked grim, not very confident. But he made no protest. The arguments were long over.

"The simulation checks out," said Phila. She shut off her list and tossed it aside. "Time for the real thing. Commander?"

Kelly resumed his seat. There was no safety harness. He felt naked. Rubbing moist palms across his thighs, he steadied himself.

"Secure the ship for takeoff," he said.

Phila reached out and activated the dozens of binary messages that flashed through the City in nanoseconds, giving commands that locked all mobile robots into place, shutting down gravity, heat, and air to non-essential areas, closing stress bulkheads at key points, switching off all teleport grids.

"Ship secure, sir."

"All right," said Kelly. "Warm the engines, Mr. Siggerson."

"Engines warming."

Back after they first realized the ship was truly theirs, Kelly and Siggerson had teleported to the engine room. Even now Kelly remained in awe of what he had seen. He could not describe it, for the technology was incomprehensible to him. Long, sleek tubes where the power mix took place. A vast tank sealed with a transparent lid containing a dark blue sludge no one could identify although Siggerson guessed it was some kind of organic coolant. A little too genetically similar to the Visci for Kelly to feel comfortable close to it. Row after row of generators feeding ship power into life support systems, which they guessed had been supplied for Holborn's research team. It was amazing how life support was supplied effortlessly to every corner of the City although the robots did not need it. Certainly the Visci themselves had not.

Matter coils as massive as Kelly's waist fed through the bowels of the ship. They had not taken the time to trace them all the way to the drive units.

"Drive units show nominal energy levels," said Siggerson now as he hunched over his control panel. "Rapidly achieving complete mass. Ready for . . . cast off?"

Kelly almost laughed. They weren't docked, yet the formal term seemed best. What else was there to say? Ready to move?

Lips quirking, he said, "Cast off, Mr. Siggerson."

"Aye, sir."

Phila caught Kelly's eye. They both smiled. Siggerson's intense expression did not change. He was sweating a bit. The responsibility for the correct navigational calculations rested on his bony shoulders. He looked nervous.

"How long a run do we need before we can jump?" asked Kelly. He had asked it before but he kept forgetting. Maybe he was nervous too.

Siggerson didn't seem to mind answering. "My estimates are that we need to attain a speed equivalent to TD 8. The course is already laid in, but you do realize, Kelly, that this ship's massive power is designed to open gates, not propel her through them. I don't think—"

Kelly raised his hand. "Go, Siggerson."

With a sigh Siggerson complied. There came an almost subliminal rumble through the ship.

"Under way, sir," reported Phila. Her voice rang out with excitement.

Kelly glanced at her. He observed her glowing eyes and the renewed quickness of her movements. She'd be all right. Healing was coming already.

Siggerson had no less than twenty specialized computers assisting him in piloting this behemoth. Her immense mass demanded constant, infinitesimal course corrections to keep her stable.

Kelly sat back in his chair and tried to look calm although his nerves kept twitching. An eternity passed while they picked up speed. She was slow, as slow as the eons, yet imperceptibly she accelerated. Smooth, powerful, gaining in her own majestic fashion, she took an hour to reach TD 8.

Eight, thought Kelly. The symbol of infinity.

He turned his head. "Launch log buoy."

"Launching log buoy," replied Phila.

If they failed to jump the time barrier, two thousand years from now perhaps someone would find this record of their attempt to get home.

Kelly reopened the line to Beaulieu. "Make ready, Doctor. We're about to jump."

"There's no change," she said, although this time he did not ask. "Take us home, Commander."

Kelly glanced at Siggerson. The pilot's face was tense with strain. He had worked the calculations a dozen times at least, wanting to make no errors with an unfamiliar system of computations he barely understood.

"Boosting," Siggerson said. "The computers will take it now. I still don't know if we can do more than open the gate. And if anyone is on the other side . . ."

"Do it," said Kelly, and braced himself.

Siggerson switched over to full automated. The City shuddered her full length, and Kelly saw indicators reflect a massive powering up. The lights flickered and dimmed.

"Gate opening one kilometer dead ahead," said Siggerson excitedly. "I hope to God it's the right time."

"Put her on the loop," said Kelly.

Siggerson's hand stretched out, curled with hesitation, then touched the necessary controls.

The lights went out completely. A force slammed Kelly in the chest. His cry of pain remained muffled in his throat for he had not the air to express it. The ship seemed to be whirling about him, spinning madly on her axis until he was flattened and thinned to a thread of existence in the centrifugal lash. He saw a blur of colors, dazzling across the full spectrum, flowing into him with beauty too exquisite to comprehend. His own shape blended with them so that he became color too. And he had no existence save this river rushing forever between the banks of infinity. His mind never lost consciousness as it had before. He felt the calmness of center. He saw the links and connections of life itself. He understood the greatness of creation, recognized the limitless combinations and possibilities. Awe filled him. It was so simple, so perfect, so beautiful.

Slowly . . . slowly the spinning lessened. The colors ceased to blend. They separated, became distinct and harsher in definition. He lost them, lost sight as well, and with it his comprehension, his calmness—all of it flowing away from him despite his efforts to cling to it. He might as well have tried to hold water in his hand.

The City's power drives deaccelerated fraction by fraction, as smoothly as she had accelerated. Magnificent, immense, her hull shining as black and sleek as the day she was built—she shimmered through the time gate of her own making and let it close behind her, cutting off the loop of time.

At last the City sailed to a dead stop, resting in space precisely fourteen meters from her departure point. Her automateds switched over to new relays, shutting down the massive power coils, and restoring partial control to the manuals of helm and navigation. She purred at ready, waiting for new commands.

Within her, all lay still.

"Hailing unidentified ship. Hailing unidentified ship. Please respond. This is the ESS *Hoyt* calling. We have peaceful intent. Please respond."

The message was repeated over and over in a multitude of major languages, cycling from Glish Standard to Minzanese Prime to Saluk to mathematical symbols. It came over the speakers attuned to outside frequencies.

At last it roused Kelly. He blinked and with an effort lifted his head. It felt like a five-ton rock balanced on the end of his neck. He listened a moment without comprehension, then slowly the words became clear.

A smile spread across his face. He lifted his hands and peered at them, flexing them to test their solidity. Then eagerly he switched on the scanners and examined a formation of Alliance ships at a cautious range of nine thousand kilometers. They looked tiny in proportion to the City.

He opened a hailing frequency and spoke in Glish. "This is Commander Bryan Kelly of the . . ." He hesitated a moment. What had her owners called her? What Visci name had christened her? He would never know. "This is Commander Bryan Kelly of the *City*. We have peaceful intent."

A request for visual came across. Kelly glanced at Siggerson and Phila, both still unconscious. He complied, and as the bridge of the *Hoyt* shimmered upon his screen, he could hear whoops and cheers in the background. A human face stared at him.

"I'm Captain Komaki. Are you Kelly of the Star-Hawks?"

"That's right," said Kelly, grinning even more broadly.

Komaki whistled. "What the hell kind of ship are you in? I've never seen anything that big in my life."

"It's a Visci configuration," said Kelly casually. "Are you going to escort us home?"

"Uh, yeah. I guess so. Admiral Jedderson and Commodore West request permission to beam aboard. Is that vessel secure?"

"Yes," said Kelly, straightening hurriedly. "Stand by for confirmation, *Hoyt*."

He snapped off the visual and left his seat.

He intended to go to Siggerson and Phila to awaken them. But his legs were unexpectedly jellified. He staggered and nearly fell. By then, however, Siggerson was groaning and coming around.

"Are we there?" he asked without opening his eyes.

"Yes," said Kelly. He took a more cautious step this time.

"Smooth ride," said Siggerson. "I don't remember a thing. What are you doing?"

Kelly smiled at him. "Trying to get my space legs back. Smooth or not, I don't think man was intended for time travel. Wake up Phila, will you? We're about to be boarded and I want us at least able to make sense."

"Boarded? By whom?"

"Our boss."

"Who?"

Kelly frowned. Siggerson was never going to fit in Special Operations. He remained too civilian, too indifferent, even down to who he worked for. "Jedderson," said Kelly impatiently. "Fleet-Admiral Jedderson. The founder of the Hawks, now—"

"Yes, yes. I know who he is. Commander in chief of all Allied forces." Siggerson rubbed his face and blinked to put himself in focus. "How'd he get here?"

"We're *there*, Siggerson. We made it. Take a look at the scanners. A whole flotilla is sitting off our port side."

A smile, perhaps the first genuinely warm, excited smile Kelly had ever seen from him, flashed across Siggerson's face. He pulled himself woozily to his feet. "Damn! Are they? I can't believe it."

In his excitement he stuck out his hand to Kelly. A little surprised, but delighted, Kelly shook it firmly.

Siggerson ran his hands through his thinning hair, making it stick straight out. He laughed. "What a ship. I don't understand a third of her controls. I never thought we could do it."

"Well, we did do it. And Jedderson is coming aboard."

"Right. Shall I pick up the coffee cups and swab the deck?"

"Just switch systems back on," said Kelly around a smile. "I'm going down to check on Beaulieu."

Ouoji bounded after Kelly as he left central control. By the time he reached the first teleport grid, it was operative. Picking up Ouoji, Kelly stepped onto it and had himself flashed to the genetics lab.

Beaulieu wasn't there. Ouoji jumped down and streaked out of sight on some purpose of her own. Kelly found Caesar sleeping beneath the sedative of a drug patch on his throat. His round, snub-nosed face had lost its gray pallor. Gently Kelly smoothed back Caesar's unruly hair and smiled down at him.

41's bunk, however, was empty. Ouoji paced back and forth along it, switching her tail. For a moment Kelly's heart stopped beating. His mind raced behind a nameless dread. Then he saw the broken restraints, and he could draw breath again.

"Find him, Ouoji."

She jumped off the bunk and made a small, searching circle. When she chittered, Kelly came hurrying.

41 sat curled in a corner behind an overturned chair. His hands were clamped upon the back of his head; his face was buried against his knees. Kelly gently moved the chair aside. He reached out to grasp 41's shoulder, but Ouoji got in the way with a warning switch of her tail.

Kelly crouched on his heels. Inside, little pulses of hope

kept bursting against his breastbone. He tried, however, to heed Ouoji and not rush things.

"41," he said gently. Now he really did wish he knew 41's name, especially whatever 41's beloved Old Ones had called him. The number itself was a buffer, an act of defiance against convention, a barricade that no one could cross. What had 41 said once? That his name had been taken from him so many times he had vowed never to wear a name again. Sad.

"41, it's Kelly. I'm here. 41?"

No response. 41 looked frozen in that position, fetal. Kelly sighed, feeling helpless. Needing comfort himself, he glanced at Ouoji. If 41 could never be reached, then . . .

Tears shimmered in Kelly's eyes.

Ouoji chittered softly. She came to him as softly as smoke and sat up on her haunches to place her paw upon his face.

Comfort flowed into him, blunting the sharp edge of grief. As soon as he realized what was happening, Kelly drew back in startlement. The contact broke immediately. He stared into Ouoji's blue eyes.

"Empathic?" he said softly.

Her eyes shone as blue as Earth's sky. She dropped to all four feet and padded to 41. She touched him, and he jerked violently, his arms flailing. Ouoji was knocked tumbling. Kelly reached out to roll her onto her feet. Beneath her soft fur, he could feel her sturdy body tremble.

41 glared wildly at them without recognition. Terror filled his face.

"Don't be afraid," said Kelly with a hand still upon Ouoji. "No one is going to hurt you."

41 bared his teeth. Ouoji moved toward him, and he pressed himself deeper into the corner. A feral noise rumbled in his throat.

"Ouoji, careful," said Kelly in alarm.

The tip of her tail crooked, but still she went toward 41. He screamed at her, the sound so bestial a chill ran up

Kelly's spine. Ouoji sprang, and 41 thrashed in an effort to fight her off. But she clung to him until she could wrap her tail around his throat. 41 froze, so tense Kelly could see him tremble. The whites showed all the way around his irises.

Keeping her tail around his throat, Ouoji pressed both her forepaws to his cheeks.

"No." The word was guttural. 41 shook his head, shuddering. "No!"

Ouoji did not desist. After a moment 41's eyes sagged closed. The tension faded from his body. Kelly held his breath, hoping she could do something, praying she could do enough to bring 41 within reach.

Ouoji removed one paw from 41's face and glanced at Kelly. He edged closer until he was beside her. She mewed almost silently at him and put her paw against his cheek.

At once Kelly felt the link. He stiffened, but overcame his instinctive resistance. If it would help 41, he had to try it.

For a moment his mind was awash with totally alien images. Dimly he recognized them as belonging to Ouoji. But before he could begin to decipher any of them, they faded away as though she blocked them from him. He touched instead a cry for help.

41's cry.

Concerned, Kelly tried to reach out to him. He wished he had genuine psionic ability, wished he knew even some rudimentary techniques.

He passed through a flaming curtain that tried to enfold him. Gasping, he broke free of it and found himself looking at a world unknown to him, a world so vast, so wide and flat it seemed too great to comprehend. Over him burned a sun like white fire, with light so clear it cut edges into him and etched his shadow with precision. A wind like song blew against his cheeks and ruffled his hair. It brought scents to him, alien scents. Some were sweet, others acrid. Plants, game spoor, the pale powdery soil itself, all mingled their fragrances within his nostrils.

A shadow flew over him. He looked up and saw a great winged creature sailing the skies, circling him. It gave a mournful, haunting cry, and he felt strange urges stir in his blood. He ran, chasing the winged one as it flew above him. He ran effortlessly, skimming the ground, with lungs and legs that never gave out. He ran until he laughed and flung out his arms, trying to fly, trying to follow the winged one as it flashed through the sky and left him.

It was the world of the Old Ones, Kelly realized while the images continued to flood his mind. The place of 41's early childhood. The place where he had been happy.

Were the Old Ones Svetzin? Was it possible?

The images darkened. The air became cool enough to make him shiver. He entered a place of stone and silence, a place that smelled old, a place where dampness seeped slowly to form deep, bottomless pools of sacred water. He sat, alone for the first time in this place of the Old Ones, and felt small. The Old Ones touched him, and he flinched. They had always been gentle, but their touch remained ever to him as a brand searing his mind, hurting him although he knew they meant him no harm. Afterward, he lay a long time upon his face, weeping. And when the next time came, the pain was just as strong, and he wept again, shamed that he should fail.

Yet their touch left knowledge in his mind each time. It was his education, formed bit by tiny bit within the compartments of his brain. After a time he understood the pain and knew he was not a species designed to learn in the way of the Old Ones. Yet they had no other means by which to care for him. Their patience was great; each lesson was infinitely small. He grew and he learned. In time the pain became a normal thing, something almost to be ignored because it was so familiar. He learned not to flinch, not to cry.

Those images faded too, and Kelly found himself in nothing. He realized in a way that the link remained, but nothing crossed. What was Ouoji doing?

Then old memories of his own filled his mind. Sensations first: gentle hands rubbing oil into his baby skin, a voice crooning him to sleep, sunshine with the double shadows of the Irani binary system. Running after Drew while their laughter echoed through the garden. Eating chocolate by putting a square upon their tongues and letting it melt across their taste buds. Stalking Kevalyn through the shadows of the house until she screamed, convinced a ghost was haunting her.

Sharing, Kelly realized. Ouoji was pulling their minds together, back and forth, equally.

He wept for the death of his sunshun, Pablo. Streaked black with age, fur turned coarse and brittle, Pablo feebly licked his hand and died.

His parents, proud and dressed in their finery, bringing the new baby home to be examined by Drew, Kevalyn, and him. Her face was tiny. He stared at the dark lashes upon her soft cheek, at the fierce tuft of hair upon her head. She smelled of lavender and they let him hold her first.

Again the images faded to darkness. Kelly waited a long time, afraid to move, becoming aware of the hardness of the floor and Ouoji's soft paw upon his skin. Had the link broken?

Kelly saw himself and was startled. Was he that tall, that fit? It was night upon a world of snow and ice. He moved through tall drifts in a clumsy, zigzagging pattern. His black hair absorbed the moonlight; his face reflected it.

The image blanked, returning to a bar filled with gritty smoke and flickering holos at every table, according to the customer's fancy. A bar on the down side of town, unrestricted, filled with dangerous types that watched for the entrance of the unwary. He sat, absorbing the fear scents of the skinny, mud-colored informer beside him while Ultan made the deal in the back room. It was his job to guard the door to that room. He sat, his chair tilted back so that his head touched the wall. A heavy pulse cannon lay across his thighs. His finger curled negligently around the trigger. He had no feelings. He simply watched, knowing that if Ultan made the deal they would have work. And work meant the chance to die for money.

"41," whispered Kelly, wanting to back away from that terrible loneliness that was like acid in the soul. He did not want to share such emptiness.

Another image came from 41: the pool, racing through water as warm as silk, laughter in his soul.

"Kel-lee."

41's voice snapped the link. Ouoji's paw dropped. Kelly's eyes opened. He stared at 41's face anxiously, hoping this had been enough. Ouoji unwound her tail from about 41's throat and jumped off his chest. Kelly took his hand, willing 41 to open his eyes and know him once again.

"41, Maon is dead," he said. "It can't hurt you again. You're safe. You're home with us. 41, this is Kelly. I'm here with you. I'm here."

41's eyes flickered open. They were dull, tired, but they focused upon Kelly's face. Awareness filled them, and Kelly could not breathe for fear the moment would fail. 41 searched his face, then he frowned. Kelly saw the pain of remembrance come. His grip tightened upon 41's hand.

"Maon is dead. It's gone from you."

"Kel-lee."

"Yes?"

"I could not . . . fight it."

"But you did fight it," said Kelly gently. "You kept Maon from killing the rest of us. You distracted it and gave us the chance to defeat it. You did well, 41. You did very well."

A faint gleam lit 41's eyes for a moment. He seemed almost to smile. "I'm . . . tired."

"Sleep," said Kelly. "It's safe to sleep. You're home."

"Does not smell like . . . home."

Kelly wondered if he meant Station 4 or the nameless world of the Old Ones. Kelly smiled, caught somewhere between a laugh and tears of relief.

"You're home, whether it smells like it or not. Trust me."

"I trust you, Kelly." 41 mumbled something else and let his eyes fall closed.

Kelly gathered him up and managed to carry him back to his bunk. He spread the blanket over him and watched him sleep for a moment. Fatigue dragged at Kelly's mind. He glanced at Ouoji and at that moment there was nothing he wouldn't have done for her.

"Thank you," he said quietly.

She chittered smugly and butted his leg with her head. *Do not tell the others about me.*

Kelly met her gaze. "I won't," he promised.

Still, it was not a homecoming to celebrate. He had his squad although Caesar clung to life by a stubborn thread, 41 looked too fragile to touch, Phila ached inside the hell of guilt, and Siggerson would probably quit the Hawks as soon as they returned to base. They had gone out unprepared; their return was a miracle.

The admiral and over two thousand crew and officers, however, would have no homecoming save a memorial.

Kelly bowed his head.

"Kelly," said Beaulieu's deep voice.

He started and looked away, keeping his face averted until he had control of his emotions once again. Then he turned to her and blinked, stunned at the sight of his father standing in the doorway beside her.

Kelly took a half step forward. "Dad."

His joy bubbled up, only to choke in his throat. He stood locked in place, unable to go to him, unable to accept the idea that death could be cheated.

The admiral stood there wrapped in a silver thermal blanket, naked otherwise. His gray hair was rumpled and damp, curling as though he had just stepped from his bath. His skin glowed a soft, pearly pink. The pink of new skin, baby skin.

Fresh from the vat.

Kelly's throat swelled. He swallowed hard, forcing down

the lump. He couldn't stand this, couldn't stand looking at him and wanting to run to his father's arms to feel the warm solidity of his father's body against his. He couldn't stand knowing that his father's—no, this *copy's*—mind was as blank as an unused data tape.

"Son?"

Kelly flinched at that voice. The tone was exactly right: rueful, slightly amused, warm.

"Aren't you going to give the old man a hug?"

Kelly shook his head, not in refusal but in denial. Yet the copy's blue eyes were keen, intelligent, aware. Not blank. A sudden hope ballooned in Kelly so fast it hurt.

He glanced at Beaulieu. She looked smug.

"First batch finished and out, dripping tracks all over the place," she said. "I never thought the process would be this fast. I forgot all about collecting clothing. I guess they'll have to raid the destroyers in their birthday suits. Which perhaps is appropriate. The admiral, however, insisted on a blanket."

"Dignity of the rank," said the copy.

Only he wasn't just a copy. Kelly couldn't keep holding the comparison in his mind. His father was back, just as though he'd never left.

"Dad," he whispered, tears welling up in his eyes. "*Dad.*"

"That's right," said the admiral. "Oh, I'm missing a few scars here and there but otherwise I'm just about the same. Your mother won't mind, I daresay, unless she decides I have younger skin than hers. Maybe we can open a spa and make a fortune to supplement our military pensions. Think so?"

Kelly laughed. He rushed forward and embraced the old man hard. The admiral squeezed him back and thumped him on the shoulder. When they parted, both of them were misty in the eyes.

"I'm glad," Kelly said, too choked up to say what he really meant. "I'm just *glad.*"

Beaulieu cleared her throat. "Well, Commander. You're welcome."

Kelly went to her and kissed her cheek, making her chocolate skin flush darker. "Thank you," he said. "I guess I was wrong."

She smiled and slipped something into his hand. Its label marked it as Visci DNA. Kelly frowned and put it in his pocket. Not total extinction, after all, for Maon's kind. Someday, perhaps humans could face the Visci again.

Beaulieu went to check on her patients, leaving Kelly and the admiral alone.

They stood there in awkward silence. "Dad," began Kelly at last. "I didn't want to try the . . . oh, hell. Do you know what happened to you?"

"Do you mean am I aware that my original self is dead and that I'm a copy?" said the admiral in a tone that put shivers through Kelly. "Yes, son. I am."

Kelly looked away, wishing he'd never brought it up. "How—how do you feel about it? I mean—"

"I don't know." The admiral gazed into the distance, wondering, sober. "I suppose I ought to be afraid. I keep pinching myself to be sure I didn't dream this. My mind tells me what happened, but I can't emotionally believe it. I don't *feel* any different. I don't *feel* like a copy. I feel like I had a damned fine bath. That's all."

Kelly drew a breath and made a decision. "Then let's think of it as just that. You're the same."

"I don't know what the ramifications are of this technology," said the admiral. "Moral and medical. Maybe this is a way to live forever. I don't want to touch any of those questions with a ten-foot pole. I don't want to tell Elizabeth or your brothers and sisters. I don't want to see in their eyes the look that you first gave me."

Shame burned through Kelly. "I'm sorry."

"Son." The admiral gripped his shoulder. "You've always been the least predictable of my children. Oh, Kevalyn is always getting herself into messes out of some stupid urge to defy me. But even that is as predictable as a book. Drew is solid, like his mother. Nothing fazes him. Nothing fires him up, either. J.J. is all spunk and no stamina. But you, Bryan, you've carved your own path. You always have, although it's cost you. I know what the others will do when they know the truth. But you're the one I really have to face."

"Dad, I—"

"We can't keep it a secret forever. The Fleet will sit on this until they decide what to do with it. Then—"

"You're still my father," said Kelly. "I've been around this galaxy enough times to see some pretty strange things. I can handle it . . . if you can."

The admiral's eyes got wet. "You mean that?"

"I mean it," said Kelly.

The admiral put out his hand, and Kelly shook it. A smile touched his lips and widened.

"Hell," said the admiral, wiping his eyes. "You got a handkerchief?"

The comm buzzed. Siggerson's stubbled face showed on the screen. "Kelly, have you got things together yet? The *Hoyt* is getting impatient."

"Tell them to wait ten more minutes," said Kelly.

"How am I supposed to tell Fleet-Admiral Jedderson to wait?" asked Siggerson.

"Be diplomatic," said Kelly with a grin. "Have Phila assemble about three hundred robots at the central teleport grid. We may as well put on a show."

Siggerson raised his brows appreciatively. "I see. Do you want carriers or fighters?"

"Make it half and half. We don't want to scare the landing party with too large a force."

Siggerson turned to relay the order to Phila, then glanced back. "This wouldn't be showing off in order to get us a new ship, would it, Kelly?"

Kelly's lips quirked. "What makes you think such a thing, Mr. Siggerson?"

"Oh, just a rumor I heard once that Fleet-Admiral Jedderson is not easily impressed. And Commodore West is notoriously tight when it comes to replacing equipment. After all," continued Siggerson, "I have my reenlistment to consider."

"I think that if we don't get a new ship to replace the *Valiant*," said Kelly, "we can probably just keep this one. Salvage rights are ours. Prize money if we want to sell her. My father has already suggested we open a spa. We could get Caesar to run the casino and—"

"—41 to be the bouncer. Right," said Siggerson dryly, but with a gleam in his eyes. "Let's make it three hundred robots of each kind. They'll fit if we teleport the landing party to the holding area where the prisoners were kept."

"Look, son," broke in the admiral, "you run Jedderson and West through hoops if you want. But while I may be a little damp behind the ears I sure as blazes haven't forgotten that you lost your ship saving my hide. The *Valiant* will be replaced. That's a promise."

Siggerson's whoop nearly shook the speaker. "I will never make insulting cracks about your having an admiral for a father again," he said fervently.

"Thank you," said Kelly.

"Me either," chimed in Phila.

"Thank *you*."

"Now," said Siggerson eagerly, his fatigue dropping away. "What are your precise orders? Would you like the robots to put on maneuvers? We could rotate the City, or—"

"Just bring the landing party over," said Kelly hastily.

"Whatever you say . . . boss."

It took Kelly a moment to absorb what he'd said. He stared at Siggerson, who was smiling a bit defiantly, a bit shyly. Kelly knew then that never again would Siggerson be outside the team. He would probably continue to grumble and drive them all nuts with his fussy attention to details, but he was one of them now.

"I'll relay the teleport coordinates to the *Hoyt* now."

Kelly's smile faded slightly. "Whoa! Let me shave first."

"And me!" said the admiral. "Damn! I've got to be in something besides a blanket if Jedderson's here."

"You can borrow 41's uniform," said Beaulieu, returning. "It won't fit very well, but—"

"Yes, that will do," said the admiral. "Wearing the wrong uniform is better than none at all. You may give my blanket to Captain Serula. Why you chose to put her in a batch with all men is beyond my understanding."

Beaulieu raised her brows while Kelly used a lab knife cautiously to scrape his chin. His ancestors must have been crazy to shave like this all the time. He nicked himself and swore.

"Men," said Beaulieu. "All vanity and very little sense of humor."

"Women," retorted the admiral. "Far too smug and clever for their own good."

Beaulieu met Kelly's gaze with a smile that held a question. "Satisfied, Commander? Will he do?"

"He'll do," said Kelly, and smiled as he gave her a thumbs-up.